# Wynter and the Stone Dragon

*Rings of Power*

**S.E. Smith**

# Acknowledgments

I would like to thank my husband, Steve, for believing in me and being proud enough of me to give me the courage to follow my dream. I would also like to give a special thank you to my sister and best friend, Linda, who not only encouraged me to write, but who also read the manuscript. Also, to my other friends who believe in me: Julie, Jackie, Christel, Sally, Jolanda, Lisa, Laurelle, Debbie, and Narelle. The girls that keep me going!

And a special thanks to Allison River, Bethanne Reid, Paul Heitsch, David Brenin, Samantha Cook, Suzanne Elise Freeman, PJ Ochlan, Vincent Fallow, L. Sophie Helbig, and Hope Newhouse—the outstanding voices behind my audiobooks!

– S. E. Smith

Summary: A powerful mage and her pet dragon cross the universe to
find the man she is destined to love and protect.

ISBN: 978-1-959584-19-3 (Paperback):
ISBN: 978-1-959584-18-6 (eBook):

{Romance – Action/Adventure – Fantasy – Paranormal}

Published by Montana Publishing, LLC
& SE Smith of Florida Inc. www.sesmithfl.com

# Contents

# Synopsis

**When a doorway between worlds opens and unites two lives, anything is possible…**

Since she was a child, Wynter Stormhold's curious nature has taken her to far-off worlds. In one world, she touches the life of a young human boy. In another, she finds her most trusted friend, a stone dragon she calls Pow-pow. Hiding her growing powers from her mage family started out as a childish prank, but now she uses them to go on secret adventures.

Sheikh Khalid el Amid's life changes forever when he encounters a beautiful but alien girl. Wynter brings unexpected miracles during his darkest hour and he vows to always protect her—but then she disappears through a portal.

When grown-up Wynter suddenly reappears years later, Khalid falls in love. All too soon, however, she is ripped from him again. As Wynter and Pow-pow fight for their lives against a mage who would use Wynter and her father's Rings of Power to control the vast worlds across space, Khalid fights for his people and his rightful place on Earth.

Can an alien princess and her dragon find her way back to her beloved sheikh, or will their responsibilities keep them apart forever?

*Previously released in Pets in Space 7! Thank you to everyone who supported the Hero Dogs charity. Together, we make a difference!

# Prologue

Arastan Stormhold cradled the newborn in his arms. Dread weighed on his heart as he looked at the alien world through the fiery, gold ring. The balcony doors of the bedroom were open, giving a view of an alien hoard overrunning the defenses of the castle.

An attacker burst into the room and the newborn's mother surged up from her bed and met the threat with a gesture that crackled with magic. When the mother collapsed back onto the bed, her features pale, Arastan watched with growing horror as the life drained from her stunning green eyes.

"Protect her."

The haunting plea washed over Arastan before he quickly closed the connection between the two worlds. No one but the baby would be coming through to Zelos.

The gold ring that used to be the portal fell to the ground, smaller than his palm once more. He partially turned when Lyia, his beautiful wife, hesitated in the doorway to his lab. Her astonished eyes were locked on the infant in his arms.

"Arastan? Where? What? Oh, my love, she is beautiful," Lyia whispered, walking forward to tenderly caress the baby's soft, platinum blonde hair that was streaked with brilliant blue strands.

Lyia glanced back at where the fiery portal had been only seconds ago, her face conveying her awe and trepidation. "How is this possible?"

The Rings of Power had never been used this way. Arastan hadn't known it was *possible* to make a traversable portal with the rings. This was not the intended result of his experiment, not at all.

He looked at the newborn in his arms, mesmerized by her brilliant green eyes. She stared up at him with a curious, trusting expression. Arastan smiled when she yawned and closed her eyes.

"I'm not sure how this is possible, Lyia, but it happened," Arastan finally replied.

"Let me take her," Lyia said.

Arastan tenderly handed the infant to his beloved wife. She beamed at the baby and stroked her cheek lovingly. Lyia had always loved children. Their unusually large family was mostly her idea. He would give her anything, and she had given him so much in return— a love and a life that he had not known could bring so much happiness.

A realization made him suddenly go cold. If the Mage Council discovered the unexpected consequences of his experiments, they could shut down his life's work. The rings were designed to allow observation, not act as a method of travel.

"No one must know about this, Lyia," Arastan warned, cupping his wife's cheek in his large palm.

Lyia nodded. "What shall we tell the others?"

"That she is our daughter. Luckily, you and the children have only recently returned from Isotope and everyone knows your love of taking in strays. They will not question it."

The sleeping infant did look Glacian enough that they could pretend she was a native of the ice world. Her skin did not have the iconic bluish tint, but not all Glacians had that coloring.

Lyia nodded before looking at him with concern. "Her family?"

Arastan shook his head. "Gone. Her mother begged me to protect her, and we will," he vowed.

"Wynter," Lyia said as she carefully made her way to the exit. "We will call her Wynter."

Arastan looked ruefully at the thick frost that coated his entire lab and smiled at how well the name fit. Ice crystals covered the surface of his workbench and the vast array of tomes that lined his walls. Icicles hung from the shelves.

He picked up the glowing ring and pulled the magical energy back into his body. The dull yellow gold reflected the stone interior of his workroom again.

He had created these rings so he could unobtrusively observe other worlds without having to travel to them. The research base they resided in was also inconspicuous. It had extremely modern conveniences, but it looked like a medieval castle. All Enyoan bases were built to blend in with the local environment. The Mage-line demanded that they observe and, if necessary, provide only the smallest amount of guidance to the worlds they visit.

The purpose of the Mage-line was to pursue knowledge and evolve, not to gain power or wealth. There were enough species in the universe who desired such things; the Mage-line would not contribute to those travesties. Mages who abused their powers were stripped of their magic and cast into a place where they were sure to die without it.

For the last ten years, he, Lyia, and their four children, Castor, Harmonia, and twins, Ladon and Electra had made a home here. The locals had accepted them, and the Mage Council had left him alone, seemingly forgetting that he and Lyia existed. The family seldom left the research base. Lyia's trip to Isotope to visit her sister was one of the rare times they were separated.

Arastan walked over to his workbench, sat down, and placed the ring next to the tome he was working on. He picked up a quill pen, dipped it into an enchanted inkwell, and began to work with a feverish intensity. Page after page filled with the scenes he had witnessed, down to the smallest detail. His ink-stained fingers trembled as he completed the final stroke. It took hours to complete, but at last he was done.

Arastan studied the finished illustrations. Confident the ink was dry, he placed the gold Ring of Power on the page. He felt determination and grief as he studied the still features of the mysterious young woman who would never again see her newborn daughter.

*This world I have just discovered is too dangerous to access again. This story is best left alone,* he sadly thought, closing the book and sealing the ring inside.

# Chapter One

"Wynter! Where are you, love?"

Four-year-old Wynter giggled and scooted under the long table in her father's lab. She loved to play hide-and-seek with her mother. Arastan, sitting at his desk along the wall, chuckled and shook his head in amusement.

"Shh!" Wynter pleaded, her eyes widening at the telltale sound of her mother's boots on the stone floor.

"Arastan, have you seen your mischievous little Movian bear cub? It is time for her bath, and she seems to have escaped again."

Wynter covered her mouth with both of her hands to smother her fit of giggles. She pulled her legs up, trying to make herself smaller. Through the legs of her father's favorite stool, she saw the hem of her mother's silver tunic.

"No, love, I haven't seen any Movian bear cubs in here," her father replied.

"Well, if you do, will you please let her know that I have a new story for her tonight?" her mother said with an exaggerated sigh.

"Give her ten more minutes. I'm sure she will magically appear," her father promised. He wrapped an arm around his wife, she leaned down just as he tilted his head back, and they kissed.

Wynter wiggled her nose and giggled some more. They did that a lot. They liked to kiss her and her siblings, too. As she looked down, she noticed one of her father's special gold rings on the floor. With glee, she put it in her pocket. She waited for her mother's footsteps to fade away, but a moment later, her mother crouched down and peered at her.

"Found you!" her mother proclaimed.

Wynter squealed and scrambled out from under the table. She ran to her father, throwing herself into his arms. Her mother's delighted laughter filled the room. Arastan rose from his chair and lifted her into the air.

"Fear not, my little Movian bear cub, I will save you from the evil bath witch!" her father declared.

With a flick of his wrist, a wooden sword appeared in his free hand. Wynter's mother put her hands on her hips and shook her head. Wynter buried her face against her dad's neck and vigorously nodded.

"You are not helping, Arastan," Lyia teased. "Come, love, you really need a bath. You've got twigs and bits of dried flowers stuck in your hair."

"No, stay. Pretty circles," Wynter pleaded, tears filling her eyes.

"I'll bathe her tonight," Arastan promised.

Lyia sighed, stepped closer, and kissed them both. "Don't be late for dinner again."

"We won't, will we, poppet?" her father said.

Wynter shook her head. "Not poppet, Movian bear cub," she impishly growled, curling her fingers as if they were claws.

Her mother blew them both a kiss. Wynter grinned over her father's shoulder and returned the kiss, loving how her mother's eyes softened with affection.

Wynter's ten-year-old brother, Ladon, peered through the doorframe and stuck his tongue out at her. She made a face at him.

"How about being a good girl while I finish taking these notes?"

Wynter nodded and her father sat her down on the stool. She studied the series of large golden orbs. They each showed a different world. Some planets swirled with deadly gases while others brimmed with life. She loved the worlds with life the most.

"Pretty," she said, pointing to one orb off to the side.

"Yes, it is beautiful. There are some interesting creatures that live there. Look at this one."

Wynter looked at the creature her father had drawn in his notebook. She ran her fingers across the image. Smooth stone scales heated her fingertips. While the stone the drawing depicted should be cold, it wasn't. The dark gray animal looked like a pile of rocks had been stacked to create a fierce beast that would have been very scary if Wynter wasn't distracted by the love the creature felt for the smaller one barely visible behind her front leg.

"These are stone dragons. As they age, their scales lose their roughness and become more polished. This is how we know when they are ready to breed. The little ones are chubby, and their bodies have a rougher surface. They seem to be loving, loyal, and nearly indestructible."

"Pet?" she asked, looking up at him with wide eyes.

Arastan chuckled and shook his head. "No, love. You can't pet them. We just watch over them."

Wynter stroked the illustration. Somewhere out of sight of her father's magic orb, Wynter sensed the mother stone dragon swinging her head from side to side, searching for the unexpected connection she felt through her scales. Her child looked up and sniffed the air. Wynter sent a wave of love to the dragon and her infant son. The stone dragon tilted her head and snorted with bewilderment.

*I pet you,* Wynter soothed. *We keep you safe.*

"Father, I need some help with Astra again. She's escaped her pen," Wynter's sixteen-year-old brother, Castor, said from the doorway.

"Give me a minute," Arastan grumbled. "Wynter, time to go find Harmonia. Ask her to give you a bath for me. This may take a while. Off you go, now."

Wynter nodded and held her arms up. Her father lowered her to the floor and fluffed her hair fondly. She walked to the door, but looked back in time to see her father wave his hand in a wide arc. Dozens of gold rings fell to the floor. He picked them up and dropped them into a woven basket on his workbench.

"Go to your sister, Wynter," he gently repeated.

Wynter hurried out of the room ahead of her father. She rounded the corner and paused, biting her lower lip. The sound of her father and brother's voices faded as they left the lab.

She peeked around the corner, waiting until they were outside. A smile lit up her face as she reached into the pocket of her dress and pulled out the gold ring she had discovered earlier. She liked to collect the pretty rings.

After looking down the corridor, she ran to the workbench and climbed onto the chair. She pulled the basket of discarded rings closer to her and rummaged through them until she found the ring she was looking for. With a grin, she climbed back down and hurried out of the room.

Several minutes later, she pulled a wooden box out from under her bed and placed the two gold rings inside with great care. She closed the lid of the box and wiggled her fingers over it. The box faded from sight.

"Wynter, bath time!" her mother called.

"Coming, mama!" she replied.

Two hours later, Wynter's mother was telling her that it was bed time.

"I'll take her," twelve-year-old Harmonia volunteered.

"Thank you, love," Lyia replied.

"I'll help," ten-year-old Electra said.

Wynter kissed her mother and father goodnight. Anyone who saw them would notice the stark physical differences between Wynter and the rest of her family. Where her parents and siblings had brown hair ranging from light to dark and eyes of similar variations, Wynter's curls were the color of a lightning bolt and her eyes were like emeralds. Sometimes the blue strands in her snow-white hair glowed almost as brilliantly as her eyes.

Wynter wrapped her arms around Harmonia's neck when her oldest sister picked her up and carried her. As they went to her room, she listened to her sisters chatting about the spells they were working on. She absorbed everything they were saying.

"Here you go. Do you want to see the stars?" Harmonia asked, tucking her into her bed.

Wynter eagerly nodded. Electra muttered and clapped her hands. Above, millions of tiny lights glowed. Wynter squealed with delight before snuggling down under the covers. Harmonia leaned over and kissed her cheek.

"Goodnight, Wynter. Sweet dreams."

"Goodnight, Wynter," Electra said, tickling her sides before blowing a raspberry kiss on her cheek.

"Love you, Ele," Wynter giggled.

Harmonia and Electra walked out of her bedroom. They didn't shut the door all the way behind them and their quiet conversation echoed in the cavernous hallway. She sat up, listening.

"Do you think she will ever find her powers?" Electra asked.

"I don't know. Father and Mother say it may not be something that her kind can ever do," Harmonia replied.

"Well, we'll just have to protect her if she doesn't," Electra declared.

Wynter looked up at the stars glowing on her ceiling and wiggled her fingers. Planets, moons, and comets appeared. She smiled. She liked the game she was playing with her family. No one knew she could do so much more than they could—even her mother and father. She didn't want to hurt their feelings. Besides, it was much more fun watching what they could create.

Sliding out of her bed, she wiggled her fingers again. The magical box that she kept hidden under her bed floated into her hands. She opened the box and worried her bottom lip. Which ring… which ring…

She had collected almost a dozen of the rings so far. Most of the rings were ones that had fallen to the floor or her father had discarded. A few were ones that she had especially liked and had taken to add to her collection. Every once in a while, she would exchange them. The basket in her father's office was always full of the rings.

She finally picked the one with the pretty garden. She liked it. There were all kinds of colorful flowers there. There was also water to splash in and a woman like her mama who sang in a strange language.

Wynter closed her bedroom door, then placed the ring in the center of the rug while threading a second ring on a magical chain around her neck. She concentrated on the words her father said to make the rings into windows. It was a pretty spell that he said protected the rings from being used by anyone else.

"Edr-portal."

The ring floated off the rug and expanded. With excitement, she peered at the beautiful garden on the other side. This was just one of the many places on the strange, new planet that her father had observed. It was in a place surrounded by sand but was also surprisingly lush.

It was nighttime there, but the single moon was bright. Within the garden, a long, narrow pool glowed with the moon's light. Stars similar to those Electra had created filled the sky and the pool's reflective surface, broken only by the ripples of the creatures within. Wynter clapped her hands. She liked the fishes in the water. They were fun to watch.

She slid her hands through the surface of the portal. One moment she was in her bedroom and the next she was falling to her knees on a stone path. She pushed up off the ground and wiped the front of her royal blue nightgown.

Scents of jasmine, sandalwood, and roses filled her nose. Wynter held her hand open out of habit and whispered a soft incantation. The golden portal closed and the ring fell into her hand. She touched the ring to the magical chain around her neck, and the chain was suddenly through the ring without her needing to unclasp it. Now she wouldn't lose her only way home.

Soft sobs caught her attention, and she looked around for the source. She followed the path around the reflection pool until she came to a set of marble steps.

A teenage boy who was maybe the same age as her brother Castor sat on the middle step. His thin shoulders shook as he cried. His head was bowed and his dark hair hung like a curtain around his face.

He was wearing white linen trousers and a thin blue shirt the same color as her nightgown. His feet were bare, just like hers. He had the same olive complexion she did. Next to him was a destroyed bouquet of flowers. Yellow rose petals lay scattered. The stems were split and twisted.

Wynter silently crawled up the lower steps like a jungle cat and playfully tickled his toes. The boy jumped and gasped. He frantically wiped at his face.

Wynter tickled the toes of his left foot again and giggled hopefully. Tickles always cheered her up when she felt bad. He pulled his foot away.

"Man—" he began hoarsely. He cleared his throat. "Man 'ant?" the boy demanded.

Wynter tilted her head. His language sounded the same as the singing lady's, but Wynter hadn't learned what any of the words meant yet. She held onto his knee as she climbed a step to settle next to him. She gently captured one of his tears and placed it on the end of her tongue.

Images flashed through her mind. The pretty woman who sang was lying on a bed. She was pale. Beads of sweat glistened on her brow, but she was shivering with cold. There were a lot of grown-ups around her, and they were all speaking in quiet voices. The boy had snuck in to see the woman, and she had reached for him. She had been in so much pain.

"Your mama?" she asked.

The boy frowned at her. He wiped his cheeks with the sleeves of his tunic and nodded. Wynter looked at the building behind him, then back at him.

"Min 'ayn 'atayt?" the boy asked.

Wynter frowned and studied the boy's face. She liked his eyes. They were a dark brown with long, black lashes. They were sad eyes. She didn't like that. She wanted to see him laugh, like her sisters and brothers. They were always laughing.

"She's there?" she asked, pointing to the building.

"Hi marida," he said.

Wynter huffed with frustration. She wanted to see the woman. She wanted to make the boy happy. Pushing on his knee, she pointed to the building again.

"We'll go help your mama."

The boy shook his head in confusion. "'Ayn 'umuk?" he asked with exasperation.

Wynter touched the boy's cheek, guiding him to look at the shattered bundle of flowers. He grimaced and a flush of color darkened his high cheekbones. Fresh tears made his eyes look glossy.

"Mama," she said slowly, waving her hands over the flowers and letting her magic flow.

# Chapter Two

Khalid el Amid ripped apart the bouquet he had picked for his mother, and he collapsed onto the garden steps, sobbing his heart out. Just because he was fourteen years old, nobody thought he could recognize that his mother was dying? He would be shocked if she made it through the night. And he wouldn't be there with her.

The doctor had said it would be best if Khalid left the room. He had fiercely protested, wanting to give her the flowers that he had picked, but his father had ordered him to leave in a harsh voice filled with grief.

Over the last few months, his mother's health had been rapidly declining, and no one knew why. She had lost weight and none of the tests the doctors performed explained why. Tonight, her breathing had grown more erratic, and her pallor had a tinge of grey.

A featherlight touch tickled his bare toes. His first thought was that it was a snake who would put him out of his misery, but a giggle alerted him to the little girl's presence on the step below him.

Shocking white hair framed her bright green eyes and her dimples. He pulled back when she tickled his toes a second time. Wiping at the tears on his face, he scanned the garden for her mother or father. He had never seen her before, but that meant nothing. The palace was filled with staff.

"Who—" he began hoarsely in Arabic. He cleared his throat. "Who are you?" he demanded.

The little girl tilted her head as if she were trying to understand what he was saying. She used his knee to steady herself as she climbed another step.

He gaped at her when she reached up, stole one of his tears, and then licked it from her finger. Her eyes glowed softly in the darkness, swirling through the endless variations of green.

She asked a very brief question, and her word for mother was familiar enough to guess what she was asking. *Your mother?*

He nodded.

She pointed at the building behind him. He glanced back to see what she was looking at, and she asked another short question that contained her word for mother.

"She's sick," he answered.

She roughly pushed on his knee and pointed behind him again with a determined expression. She said a short statement this time, something about his mother, though he had no idea what it was.

Frustrated, he scanned the garden again. He didn't want to deal with the little girl. He wanted to be alone in his grief. His father would be furious if he knew his son, the next King of Aethon, was crying.

"Where is your mother?" he demanded.

Instead of answering him, she touched his cheek. Khalid wanted to push her hand away, but the look in her eyes held him entranced. She applied enough pressure that he turned his head to look down at the crushed flowers. Tears burned the backs of his eyes. The flowers reminded him of his mother—broken and dying.

"Mama," the little girl said, waving her hands over the flowers.

The tattered bouquet glowed. Khalid scrambled back and stared with disbelief as the scattered petals swirled and connected, healing and opening, until they were in full bloom. The girl's eyes glowed with happiness.

He swallowed when she picked up the now beautiful bouquet with both hands and held it out to him.

"Mama," she said.

Khalid reached out and took the bundle. He was afraid to touch her, yet, he wanted to know if she was real. His mother used to tell him tales of the 'amirat khurafiat alsahra, mystical women who once rode across the sky on mighty stone dragons. It was said that the breath of the dragon could be seen in the sky at dawn and dusk. Aethon's desert sands supposedly came from the dragon's scales, worn down by time and wind until they were an ocean that his people could sail on.

"Mama," the little girl repeated, this time with a stomp of her bare foot and a jerky wave at the building.

Hope bloomed as he stared at the restored flowers. He took a deep breath and nodded. "Come, I will take you to her," he said, standing.

She slipped her hand into his and smiled. His chest expanded, and he stood a little taller. No one had ever looked at him like this before. This was the way people looked at his father when they came before him. This was the way his mother looked at his father.

"We must be quiet," he instructed, lifting the hand holding the flowers to his lips.

She giggled, then pressed her hand over her mouth and nodded. Together, they climbed the last steps and entered the palace. Their bare feet didn't make a sound as they wended their way to the Queen's chambers.

Khalid hoped they would get there in time—and he hoped she was alone. It was after midnight. Normally, only a single nurse sat with his mother. That was before she took a turn for the worse, though.

He heard the doctor and his uncle speaking, the low murmur of their voices getting louder as they got closer, and he pulled the little girl into an open doorway. They waited until the two men disappeared around the corner, then stepped out of the doorway and hurried along the corridor.

A guard stood leaning against the wall. The man's eyes were closed, and his arms were crossed as if he'd fallen asleep standing up. Khalid tiptoed past the man, glancing down at the little girl clutching his hand as they passed. She was staring at the guard with a curious expression.

He opened the door to his mother's quarters, gently pushed the little girl inside, and closed it quietly behind him. A lamp lit the living room with a soft glow. He crossed the room, motioning for the little girl to follow him.

He peeked into the room next to his mother's. The night nurse sat with her back to the door. She was wearing a pair of headphones and staring at her phone. He could see a movie playing on the screen. He closed the door.

They moved to the next door. A bedside light cast shadows in the room. Medical equipment beeped. The waves on the monitor were not as big as they had been the day before. The wires attached to his mother made his heart ache.

Khalid couldn't speak. Shortly after the doctor had ordered him away, Khalid had come back to see her, but his father, drowning in grief, had given in to Uncle Inarus's insistence that Khalid should not see his mother in this condition.

Resentment burned deep inside. His uncle's influence had grown over the last few months as the Queen grew sicker and the King became more distracted. Inarus seemed almost *happy* about it. It was there in tiny upticks at the corners of his mouth or the way his tone was just slightly insincere. Khalid hated him.

Stewing in rage and sorrow, he slowly walked over to the bed. His throat closed as grief choked him from the inside out.

Faiza opened her eyes. She looked tired, drained of life. Her beautiful spark was missing, the twinkle of love and laughter extinguished.

"Khalid," his mother whispered.

Her lips curved at the corners, but even that small gesture seemed to exhaust her. She moved her hand a fraction of an inch. He stepped closer and gently cupped her thin, frail fingers in his. Her hands were like ice. Her skin was like tissue paper.

"I brought you some flowers… from your garden," he replied.

He held the flowers up so she could see them. She tried to lift her hand, but didn't have the strength. He helped her touch one of the velvety petals.

When the bed jostled, she managed her turn her head just enough to see the little girl crawling across it to kneel next to her. She looked back at Khalid with a confused expression.

"I found her… in your garden. She… She is an *'amirat khurafiat alsahra*," he said.

"Oh, Khalid. I… love you," Faiza said, her eyes filled with tears.

"Don't cry, mama. She—"

Faiza's hand went slack in his and she closed her eyes, the tears spilling onto her cheeks. Khalid looked at the heart monitor. Her heartbeat was slowing down. He dropped the flowers onto the bed to grasp his mother's cold hand between his, willing her to get better.

The little girl said a short reassuring statement that had her word for mother in it, and she placed her hands on his mother's cheeks. The little girl's hair glowed with an inner light. Khalid tightened his grip around his mother's hand. There were bright blue strands in the *'amirat khurafiat alsahra's* hair.

White light began to flow through his mother's veins. He noticed it first in her face before it moved downward. The little girl spoke softly in her alien tongue.

Faiza's hair became more vibrant, healthier. The color of her cheeks turned richer and the planes of her face less shrunken. Khalid stared at the hand he was holding. It was no longer icy cold. His mother gripped his hand with a surprising strength. The beeping of the heart monitor grew stronger and steadier and the numbers rose before leveling out.

His mother gasped and opened her eyes. Her spark was back and she was more beautiful than ever.

# Chapter Three

Faiza touched the platinum curls of the little girl snuggled up against her side. She had woken after months of feeling ill with a startling new awareness. Shifting until she could sit up, she stared with disbelief at her son before she turned and studied the little girl who was yawning.

"Khalid?" Faiza asked, her voice filled with confusion, fear, and wonder.

"I'm here, mama. It's ok. Everything is ok now. You'll be ok."

He hugged her, managing it without jostling the sleeping child or letting go of his mother's hand. As she reached around the child to clasp her son's shoulder and stroke his cheek, Khalid's words came back to her.

*I found her in your garden. She is an 'amirat khurafiat alsahra.*

If she hadn't experienced the miracle herself, she would have dismissed her son's words as a flight of fancy. Instead, she began planning how she would protect the child.

"If she is found out, Khalid, she will not be ok. You must take her to Dhat-Badan. She must be taken away from here and hidden well. No one can know about her. If they find out what she can do, they will destroy her. You must protect her and keep her secret. No one, not even your father, must ever find out about her."

Khalid nodded, his eyes wide. "I'll take her away."

"Tell Dhat-Badan that this is a child of the desert and by the Queen's orders she must be protected at all costs. Do not tell her anything more," she instructed.

"I will, mama," he said. "I will protect her, too, I swear."

Faiza gently shook the girl's shoulder. "You must wake, child. Go with Khalid."

The little girl sat up and rubbed her eyes, then the *'amirat khurafiat alsahra* smiled joyfully and held her hand. Faiza's heart tightened with warmth and fear.

The child looked around the room with a frown, then slid off the bed and walked over to a tray that had been left on a small table. It was the soup she had been too weak to eat earlier.

The girl picked the bowl up and sniffed at it, then turned her face away with an expression of distaste. She brought the bowl over to her and Khalid, looking at them with surprisingly angry eyes.

She placed the bowl on the nightstand and wiggled her fingers over it. A noxious green gas rose from the bowl. The little girl scowled and said something in an unfamiliar language.

Faiza stared at the bowl of soup with growing horror, the pieces of the puzzle falling into place. This was why she had grown weaker and weaker for months. She slid her hand over her stomach as nausea churned.

"Go now, Khalid," she whispered, looking at her son with haunted eyes. "Keep her safe."

Khalid urged his mare into a face pace across the sands. After leaving his mother's bedroom, he had snuck the little girl back to his rooms, collected some supplies, and pulled one of his long-sleeve tunics over the girl's head to help keep her warm on their journey. His shirt was a dress on her, and she had giggled again.

Keeping her quiet as they crept to the kitchen had proved difficult, but soon he was gathering crackers, cheese, fruits, and a dozen bottles of water. The sacks were heavy by the time he was done.

Within fifteen minutes, he had saddled his beautiful Arabian mare, tied their supplies to the back of the saddle, and was lifting the little girl up.

"Thank you," he had said, staring up at her. "Thank you for saving my mama."

She had leaned over and touched his head. That was all it took for him to know that she understood him well enough in that moment and she was responding with her version of 'you're welcome'. He mounted behind her, and they set off through the palace gates that bordered the desert.

After an hour of riding, he slowed the mare to a trot. Killing his horse would not save the little girl. She yawned again. He was tired, too, but they had a long way to go.

She mumbled in a sleepy voice.

"What?" he asked, leaning forward, forgetting for a moment that he wouldn't understand her even if she spoke clearly.

She pulled on the reins, and the mare slowed to a stop. He frowned when she pointed to the ground. Shaking his head, he pointed ahead of them.

"We go that way," he said.

She repeated what she'd said, looking up at him with pleading eyes.

Khalid shook his head. "I don't understand. We have to keep going. I'll protect you. I swear on my life."

Her bottom lip trembled, and she rubbed her nose. She looked like she was about to cry before she finally relaxed and leaned back against him. Khalid breathed a sigh of relief. He clucked his tongue and the mare began walking again.

It was nearly dawn when he crested the last dune and stared down at Deion. Exhaustion nearly pulled him out of the saddle.

A group of riders approached as he descended the dune. His mare stumbled and slid on a patch of loose sand near the bottom. He regretted the exhausting pace he had forced the gentle beast to maintain.

"Soon, *siddiqui*," he promised, leaning forward enough to rub the mare's neck.

"Prince el Amid," one of the riders greeted.

Khalid looked at the woman and spoke with the same commanding tone he had heard his father use a million times. "Ayesha, I must speak with Dhat-Badan. I have an urgent message from the Queen."

"I will let her know at once, Your Highness."

With a whoop, she turned and kicked her mare into a gallop. Another rider fell into step with Khalid.

"The child is very unusual. I have never seen hair that color before," the middle-aged man commented.

"She is under my protection," Khalid said. His thin arms tightened around her.

Zaki bowed his head and smiled reassuringly.

The little girl woke as they neared the outer walls of the city. Her emerald eyes widened as she looked around. She lifted her arms above her head as she stretched, and then grinned excitedly at Wahida, a rider in her twenties. The woman laughed.

They passed through the arched stone entrance. The city was surrounded by a tall, thick stone wall. Built over a thousand years ago, the city had withstood sandstorms, invasions, drought, and famine.

They arrived, and Khalid reluctantly handed the girl to Imad, Dhat-Badan's son and Wahida's husband. He stiffly climbed off the mare, handing the reins to Wahida.

"I will take good care of your mare," Wahida promised.

"Thank you," Khalid replied.

The little girl asked something, and Khalid smiled at her when she reached for his hand. He wished he could understand her. He picked her up. His arms felt like lead, but he didn't want her walking across the ground barefoot.

"Do you wish for me to carry her, Your Highness?" Imad inquired.

"No, she is my responsibility," Khalid replied with a shake of his head. He noticed the group's curious stares, and his arms tightened protectively around the girl's slender body.

He followed Imad and Zaki. They led him to the doorway of a courtyard, and he released his hold on the little girl. She slid down his body until her feet hit the tiled floor. Off to the side, a round table with chairs occupied the space beneath lush palms. A woman in her fifties rose to her feet with a serene smile.

"Your Highness, Ayesha says the Queen has need of me," Dhat-Badan greeted with a low bow.

Khalid had met Dhat-Badan several times. She had been his mother's nanny when Faiza was a little girl. Most knew her as the Wise Woman of Deion.

"What I have to say must be said to you alone," he announced.

Dhat-Badan's eyes widened with surprise. Her eyes fell on the little girl holding his hand. She murmured to the group who had entered with them. In seconds, they were alone with Dhat-Badan. He released the little girl's hand and stepped forward.

"The girl is a child of the desert. By the Queen's orders, she must be protected at all costs," he recited.

Dhat-Badan reached out and touched the little girl's hair, instantly yanking her hand back and rubbing her fingers as if she had been shocked. Khalid wrapped his arm around the little girl's shoulders.

"Where did she come from?" Dhat-Badan inquired.

"Khalid…." the little girl interrupted, tugging on his hand.

Khalid crouched in front of her. She placed her hand on his cheek. Her eyes looked huge and glowed with that unique brilliant green color. He could see himself in their reflection.

"Khalid… Wynter glenn- bar hi," she spoke slowly, enunciating each word carefully. He realized she had said the word Wynter before… several times.

"Wynter," he repeated, touching her chest.

The little girl's face lit up, and she nodded. "Wynter glenn- bar hi," she repeated.

He still didn't understand the other words she spoke. He was about to ask her when Imad entered with a tray of refreshments. Khalid's stomach grumbled at the sight of the pastries.

"You and the child must be hungry," Imad said, placing the tray on the table before quietly retreating.

"Yes, very. Wynter, eat," Khalid offered, mimicking eating.

Wynter shook her head and turned away, walking to the center of the courtyard. A moment later, she placed something on the ground, then stood and stepped back.

"What is she doing?" Dhat-Badan asked.

Khalid lifted his shoulders. "I don't know."

Wynter smiled at them. "Wynter glenn- bar hi," she said again with a wave of her hand. "Edr- portal."

A swirling circle opened in front of her. Dhat-Badan released a startled cry and retreated behind the table while Khalid stood rooted to the spot. The portal reminded him of the story *Through the Looking Glass.*

On the other side of the round doorway was an alien world. A large volcano spewed a vast cloud of smoke in the far distance. Thick ferns in shades of red leaves rose nearly ten feet high on navy blue stems. Mounds dotted the bare ground between the ferns, reminding him of pictures in a dinosaur book that he still had at home.

Wynter stepped through the portal and in a blink of an eye, it was gone, and so was she.

Khalid's heart was pounding, and his mouth was dry. He startled when Dhat-Badan placed her trembling hand on his shoulder. He shrugged off her hand and walked to the spot where Wynter had disappeared. He turned in a slow circle as he searched the ground. When he finally stopped, he was swaying with fatigue and shock.

The last twelve hours of his life had changed him. He blinked, his eyes burning at the thought of never seeing Wynter again. Dhat-Badan walked over to him.

"She truly is a child of the desert," the woman murmured with awe.

# Chapter Four

Wynter glanced around her. She was in a barren section of ground surrounded by fern-like trees. She had used the wrong ring. She hadn't gone home, she was in the world with the stone dragons. Rubbing her eyes, she sat down on the ground. She sniffed and wiped away a tear.

"Mama… Papa," she mewed.

A noise from behind caused her to turn. A small oval-shaped stone moved back and forth, then stilled. Curiosity overrode her exhaustion, and she climbed back to her feet and walked over to the rock. It was hard to get to because it was in a wide hole with dirt mounded high around it.

She squatted down next to the rock. When it didn't move, she pushed on it with her finger. She gaped in delight when the rock rolled away from her before stopping. She stood up and walked over to it. Squatting again, she touched the rock with her finger a second time.

Wynter giggled when the rock rolled in a circle around her and stopped again. She turned and touched the rock over and over until she was dizzy. Falling down in a heap of laughter, she stared at the rock as it slowly uncurled. Brilliant emerald eyes the same color as hers stared back at her with curiosity. Slowly, the creature unfurled its body, and Wynter saw that it was a tiny stone dragon.

"Pet!" she demanded, wiggling her fingers with delight.

The stone dragon took an unsteady step toward her before its legs gave out. Wynter reached out and caressed its head. The dragon released a low purr and wound around her, nudging her. She gently scratched its chin.

The ground shook, and she jumped. The little dragon grinned, lifted its club-like tail, and struck the ground again with a resounding thump.

"Pow-pow!" Wynter exclaimed with delight.

She wrapped her arms around the dragon's neck. The dragon wagged its tail again, shaking the ground so much that Wynter's bottom bounced. She laughed and petted the dragon.

A loud, terrifying screech shattered the peaceful quiet, and they both froze. The little dragon whimpered and snuggled closer to her.

"We go home," she said in a low voice.

She scrambled to her feet, clawing her way out of the hole, and searched the ground until she saw the shimmer of gold where she had dropped one of the rings. She hurried over and picked it up just as the trees cracked and parted. The head of a massive serpent appeared through the opening, its long, forked tongue tasting the air. Vivid yellow eyes locked on the dragon before turning to focus on her.

Wynter tossed the ring into the air and thought of her nice, safe bedroom. With one hand she reached for the ring, with the other she reached for Pow-pow. The little dragon mewed in terror, caught between the serpent and the threads of blue light that were pulling it toward the portal.

In a split second, the dragon decided that the room with the colorful blankets and pretty lights was much more comforting. Tucking in its legs and head, the dragon fashioned itself into a round rock and let the blue strands pull it through the portal. Wynter scrambled through the portal, too, and closed it a split second before the serpent struck.

Tired but safely back in her bedroom, Wynter picked up the heavy baby rock dragon and pushed it up onto her bed. She pulled off the filthy tunic Khalid had given her and kicked it under her bed before she climbed up beside Pow-pow and fell onto her back. She would find Pow-pow's mother tomorrow. Touching her father's drawing would give Wynter a sense of where the older dragon was.

When Harmonia checked on her early the next morning, Wynter was sound asleep, sprawled out with her arms over her head, her platinum curls wild and tangled, and her feet very dirty. Harmonia bit her lip and studied the rock her baby sister was snuggling with. She waved her hand over Wynter, whispering a cleansing spell, and straightened the covers.

It was a good thing Harmonia didn't turn around as she exited the room. If she had, she would have seen a pair of curious eyes, almost the exact color of Wynter's, staring after her.

---

Time passed and Pow-pow became the newest member of the Stormhold family. It had taken a while for her parents to agree that Wynter could keep the rock dragon, but it was inevitable. All of Pow-pow's family was dead—a victim of the serpent. They couldn't leave the little dragon all alone.

Fortunately for Wynter, her father had been determined to discover how the dragon was able to traverse through the Ring of Power. Wynter had replaced the ring in the basket the following morning, and because of her age, none of her family suspected that she had been the one responsible. Her father was convinced he must have somehow caused the dragon's appearance in their home, and he spent months trying to replicate the conditions that would create a portal instead of a window.

Wynter's mother, on the other hand, was simply fascinated with Pow-pow. Their isolation made raising a dragon possible, and the obvious bond between Wynter and the creature had made it virtually impossible to say no.

Of course, that didn't mean that life was always rosy. Raising a growing rock dragon inside a medieval castle/Mage-line research facility was bound to have its trials. The upside was that they had no problems any longer with the large-eared rodents that used to sneak into the kitchen, or with starting a bonfire outdoors in even the dreariest weather, or with breaking through the thick exterior walls when her oldest brother discovered a sealed passage in the ruins.

The downside was—well, having a growing rock dragon with a tail that could smash through thick stone walls living indoors. Electra and Ladon's daily chore was to repair all of the damage done when Pow-pow chased the odd kangaroo mouse through the corridors or decided to wag his tail.

Then there were his wings. They sprouted when he turned eight. They were growing larger, and when he forgot to tuck them next to his body, he could split a building in half. Everyone loved the feisty dragon though.

"Come on, take me for a ride!" eighteen-year-old Wynter hollered, racing across the meadow as Pow-pow bounded after her.

Pow-pow lowered his head, catching her under her rump, and tossed her into the air as if she were a bale of hay. She came down on Pow-pow's back just in front of his wings and held onto the ridge of his spine plates as he did a few experimental jumps before unfurling his wings and lifting off.

A heady excitement filled her as the ground moved farther and farther away beneath them. Pow-pow's flight skills were incredible. She stroked a patch of rough scales.

As he grew older, he began shedding his scales. The new ones under them were smooth. The combination of rough and smooth gave him a textured appearance.

*How fast can you go?* she asked through their mental connection.

Pow-pow's mischievous, rumbling chuckle was the only warning she got before he shot upward with a breath-stealing burst. A rumble of thunder sounded a few seconds behind them, and Wynter realized that it was caused by Pow-pow breaking the sound barrier.

*No wonder I feel like I have one of your scales crushing my chest!* she shared.

*I would go faster, but it hurt you,* Pow-pow replied.

*Thank you,* she said with an affectionate pat.

Far below them, Wynter studied the swiftly moving landscape. It was half-a-day's shuttle ride to the nearest town. At the speed Pow-pow was flying, they could probably make it in half the time.

Rolling meadows surrounded the research center. Farther out was a thick forest where a variety of wild, dangerous, and beautiful creatures lived.

Wynter's mother specialized in the flora and fauna of different alien worlds and the medicinal properties of various found substances. Pow-pow was a bit of a mystery since he ate dirt and rocks instead of plants and animals. Clay was like dessert to him. He loved to dig into the riverbed. The problem was that it made him tipsy if he ate too much, which invariably led to more household damage.

In the last month, it was decided that Pow-pow would be happier and their home would be safer if he lived in his own special house. That house was a quickly constructed barn made of material that he wouldn't eat.

*Let's fly over the ocean,* Wynter requested.

Pow-pow turned to the right, over the sheer cliff walls, and floated higher on a current of wind. Wynter breathed in the fresh salty air, holding it in her lungs for as long as she could before she released it. Her long plait of platinum hair lifted on a gust of wind.

With a thought, a long coat appeared around her. Her thin white blouse and brown vest were not enough to keep out the chill from the air currents coming off the ocean.

Stretching out a hand, she formed a series of circles using water vaper. Pow-pow weaved in and out of them, enjoying the game.

*Why you still no tell your family about your magic?* Pow-pow asked.

*Why don't you talk to them like you do me?* she countered.

Pow-pow snorted and changed direction. They were heading back toward the cliffs. She sighed when Pow-pow glided in to a smooth landing, trotting several yards before he stopped. She slid off his back, walked over to the grass, and sat down.

He shook himself before neatly folding his wings against his sides. She lifted her arm and waited for him, knowing that he would trot over to her and she would put her arm over his neck. She wouldn't be able to do that much longer with the way he was growing.

Wynter looked out over the ocean. Her mind fluttered from one thought to the next. Pow-pow's words about sharing her magic ability with her parents weighed heavily on her heart. What had started out as a game when she was a baby had morphed into a habit.

Hands down, she was more powerful than her parents and siblings. She didn't understand how or why, but she knew she could do things they couldn't. That, and the fact that she looked so different from all of them…. She didn't like thinking about it. It made her uneasy. She played with the end of her long plait.

"What we doing tonight?" Pow-pow asked.

"I don't know. Maybe explore the woods again," she said with a shrug of her shoulders.

Dusk was settling around them. She and Pow-pow liked to slip out after everyone went to sleep. Sometimes they flew for miles and miles along the coast or explored the woods. Other times, she would pilfer a few of the power rings from her dad's lab and they would explore exotic worlds.

She had to be very careful when they did that. More than once, she had forgotten to invoke a glamour spell, and they were seen. In worlds that had never seen a mage riding a stone dragon, that could cause havoc. It was one of the things her father had been very vocal about over the years. The creed of the Mage-line was to observe—not interfere.

Pow-pow groaned, rolled over onto his side, and hung his tongue out of his mouth as if he were dying. Wynter laughed and pounced him, tickling his belly until he was rolling back and forth and pounding the ground with his tail. She sighed and leaned back against him, staring up at the sky.

"Life is boring now that Harmonia and the others have left," she said.

"You could visit them," Pow-pow suggested.

She caressed his nose. "Not without you. You and I… we're a team. You are safe here and so am I," she said.

*I love you, Wynter.* Pow-pow silently sent the thought to her.

"I love you, too," she said.

# Chapter Five

"Wynter, your mother and I need to visit the Mage Council for a few days," Arastan said at dinner that night.

"I thought you were still avoiding them."

Her mother smiled. "It's different now that Harmonia is working for the Council. Your father doesn't think they're idiots anymore," she said with amusement.

Wynter laughed and her father scoffed.

"The *only* smart thing they have done is give Harmonia a position," he retorted.

"I've made some meals for you. Will you be alright for a few days on your own?" her mother asked.

"Of course! And I won't be on my own. I'll have Pow-pow."

"We'll check in," her father replied, peering at her across the table.

Wynter rolled her eyes. "There is plenty to keep me busy. I've started organizing the library. That will keep me busy for a month!" she said.

Her dad shook his head. "You and your obsession with my library," he teased.

"I love every one of the worlds that you've cataloged. It is a priceless collection," Wynter said.

"Well, that should keep you out of trouble for a little while," Arastan agreed.

Two hours later, with a lot of encouragement, reassurances that she would be fine, and a little nudge, her parents departed for Wall, the closest city, to catch the red-eye shuttle to Enyo. Wynter was practically dancing by the time they left and could barely contain her excitement any longer. Pow-pow bounded out of his shelter, twirling in circles and hopping up and down.

"Where we go? Where we go?" Pow-pow impatiently demanded.

Wynter bit her lip and thought for a moment. "I don't know. Why don't I grab a couple of rings and we'll choose one at random?" she suggested.

"Not serpent place," Pow-pow warily responded.

Wynter stroked Pow-pow's nose and shook her head. "No. No serpent place. Wait here, I'll be back in a minute."

Wynter hurried back into the castle, running through the corridors until she reached her bedroom. Falling to her knees, she summoned her treasure box. It had grown over the years.

She carefully lifted the clean tunic from the box. Unconsciously, she touched the ring of power tucked between her breasts on a gold necklace. She stroked the soft material of the tunic and thought about her dreams and her memories of not just that night but the years she had watched the boy named Khalid through the portal.

Her fascination with the boy from that distant world had grown to the point of obsession. To protect herself from heartache, she had eventually forced herself to stop watching him, but she was unable to completely cut ties with him. Wearing the ring had been a compromise. It had been years since she had seen him through the portal.

In her treasure box lay the dozens of other power rings she had secretly collected over the years. She grabbed a handful and stuffed them into a small leather pouch before pulling tight the string at the top. She replaced the shirt in the box and touched the ring she wore on a necklace again. Sighing, she resealed the box and put it away.

Glancing around her room, she collected her long dark brown coat and the largest bag that she could wear draped across her chest. She exited her room and hurried down the hallway to her father's lab.

With a swift scan of the room, she found her power staff. The device was very deceptive, like all of their creations. It appeared to be only six inches long, but she could extend it by one or both ends with a thought. She pulled her coat back far enough to secure the staff at her waist.

As she turned away, her elbow caught a tome she had left on the corner of her father's workbench. She cursed when it fell to the floor. A gold power ring fell out of the book and rolled across the floor. Wynter picked the book up and placed it back on the workbench.

"Wynter, hurry!" Pow-pow grumbled.

"I'm coming," she called.

She scooped up the ring that had fallen out of the book and exited the lab. Sliding the ring into her pocket, she broke into a jog. If she didn't hurry, Pow-pow would come inside, and she would spend the next few days repairing the damage instead of having fun.

Pow-pow backed out of the doorway and wiggled his nose when he saw her. He blew a puff of hot air around her, she coughed pointedly.

"You really need to brush your teeth. Your breath smells like brimstone."

"Later. I want to have fun."

"Well, we have all the places we've been before...." she said with a cheeky expression.

Pow-pow groaned and sat down with a huff. "Or...?"

She pulled the ring out of her pocket and wiggled it between her fingers. "I found a new one. I have no idea where it goes or if we can even go there. It fell out of one of dad's tomes. How do you feel about an adventure?"

Pow-pow pranced around in a circle. Wynter would have gone flying if she hadn't leaped over his tail as it swept by her. Luckily, she was used to her friend's exuberant behavior. She laughed loudly, practically dancing herself, and then she made herself take a breath and be responsible for a second.

"Remember, no going through until we know it is safe. The last thing we want to do is walk onto a gas planet or into a star."

This time it was Pow-pow who rolled his eyes. "I know, I know."

Wynter tossed the power ring into the air and opened it with a wave of her hand. She no longer had to whisper a spell to open them. Over the years, as she became more powerful, she learned that she didn't need to say a spell out loud to make many things work. As long as she clearly imagined what she wanted, she could control the flow of power to make it happen.

The ring expanded and their reflection shimmered before the world on the other side became clear. Slowly, the excitement drained from her, leaving her feeling hollow. Pow-pow stopped bouncing and stepped closer to her.

"Wynter, I don't like this place." His voice had dropped to a deeper tone, almost a growl.

On the other side of the ring was a dark and desolate world. The open balcony doors showed ash as far as she could see. Scorched protective walls were manned by blackened bodies frozen on their feet. The walls of the room the portal had opened into were also marred by scorch marks. The furniture was broken and the room was covered in cobwebs.

A woman lay on the bed. Her features were sculpted from a fine powder. Her right arm lay out to the side as if she were reaching out to someone. She had the same long platinum blonde hair that Wynter did. It lay spread out across the dusty pillows. Her purple robe was adorned with colorful flower embroidery. Beneath the robe was a silver nightgown. While the room looked as if it had been ransacked, the woman's body remained intact.

Wynter took a step forward, and threads of white and blue energy spiked outward from the portal and wrapped around her. She screamed as the powerful bands dragged her through the magical doorway. Ancient memories shattered her mind.

"Wynter!" Pow-pow hurled himself after her a second before the portal closed.

---

**Earth: Palace of Aethon**

Khalid silently moved along the outer wall of the palace with his group of men. At twenty-eight years of age, he was the leader his father had trained him to be, and tonight, justice would finally prevail.

Life had been difficult since his mother's poisoning. His parents had become suspicious of everyone except the person they should have suspected. The truth came to light during the parade celebrating Aethon's National Day of Freedom when he was eighteen. Khalid's parents had died in a car bomb.

His uncle's plan to rule Aethon would have succeeded if his father hadn't insisted at the last minute that Khalid ride in a separate vehicle. The small force loyal to his uncle Inarus had opened fire on the procession, but Khalid's guards had whisked him away to safety.

The assassination of the beloved King and Queen had left the country in shock. Inarus had used that to take over the country—declaring himself King within hours of the murders. By law, Khalid could not assume the throne until his twenty-eighth birthday, which had passed two weeks ago.

The plan was for Khalid's largest force to enter through the main gates while he and his team entered through the rear gardens. Tonight, he and those still loyal to his parents would regain control of the country. It had been almost a decade since his parents died. The years had been long and bitter.

Khalid followed the wall to the recessed iron gate, and one of his people quietly cut the thick lock with a pair of bolt cutters. The gate creaked from disuse as he pulled it open. He winced at the sound. Stepping through the arched doorway, he scanned the overgrown foliage, angrily pushing down memories of his mother walking in the garden. She would have been singing sweetly as she trimmed her beloved roses.

He motioned for the team to move forward and sent a quick gesture to General Adham Husam to take the right fork with his team while Khalid led the other team to the left. He held his rifle firmly against his shoulder and searched the area in front of him for resistance.

They reached the steps leading up into the palace. Adham's team arrived too, and Khalid nodded to him. It was fitting that they led this charge together. Adham had been his private guard since he was a boy, and he became a close friend after Khalid's parents died.

Moving forward, Khalid stepped on something and lifted his foot, noticing the crumpled dried remains of a rose. It pulled up a memory from fourteen years ago—one he would never forget but sometimes wondered if he had imagined. The little girl with white hair who had performed a miracle. A child whose touch could heal and create a magical doorway.

His mother had never mentioned her again. If not for Faiza's miraculous recovery, Khalid would never have believed the girl truly existed.

He looked over his shoulder to see the garden, searching as he always did when he came here. After that fateful night, he could have sworn he had felt her presence here for years.

"Your Highness, is everything alright?" Adham murmured.

Khalid gave a sharp nod. Now was not the time for memories.

"Take the east wing. I'll take the left," he murmured.

Gunfire erupted, shattering the silence and chasing everything but the fight for survival from his mind.

# Chapter Six

**Through the Ring of Power: Nysus**

"Wynter, wake up," Pow-pow urged, nudging her with the tip of his nose.

Wynter didn't want to wake up. Her whole body vibrated as if she were about to explode. Power unlike anything she had ever felt before was flowing through her veins. Her hair was practically standing straight up from her head. The strands of blue pulsed.

Forcing one eyelid open, then the other, she saw straight up Pow-pow's nostril. She made a face and rolled over onto her side. The room spun.

"Wha—what happened?" she asked.

Pow-pow was curled protectively around her. As he looked around the room, she followed her dragon's gaze and noticed the absence of the white and blue lightning that had brought her here.

She stared at the bed and trembled as memories flooded through her. Holding onto Pow-pow, she pulled herself to her feet.

"I... know this place. I... remember, but I don't know how," she croaked.

Her heart hammered against her chest at the sight of a fragile woman lying on the bed. She kept one hand pressed against Pow-pow until she felt steady enough to take a step.

Next to the bed was a cradle. Dried flowers turned to dust when she touched them. Wynter watched the dust swirl, growing denser. The room changed.

Ghostly apparitions moved as if she and Pow-pow weren't there. White blossoms on a leafy-green vine adorned the cradle. An infant girl, only a few minutes old, lay sleeping in the cradle. She had an olive complexion and platinum hair. An old woman was cleaning blood from her tiny body while another tended to a woman who bore a striking resemblance to the baby. Her green eyes were identical to the child's, her complexion was only a few shades darker, and her hair was as white as snow. She lay exhausted on the bed, her face flushed, her hair soaked with sweat, and the lower half of her nightgown covered in blood.

"Larenta!"

Wynter turned as a tall man with pale skin burst through the doorway. Blood stained his clothing and dripped from his temple. He carried a long staff. Each end glowed a brilliant gold. Wynter instinctively reached for the staff at her waist. They were identical.

"Everes, you've returned! What is it? What's happened? You're hurt!" Larenta gasped, struggling to sit up.

Larenta waved her attendant away and slid from the bed. She pulled on the purple dressing gown. The man rushed toward the bed, passing right through Wynter as she attempted to stagger out of the way. Larenta swayed and would have collapsed but Everes caught her.

"You've given birth." Everes' eyes closed as if he were in pain. When he opened them, his eyes were teary before he blinked the moisture away. "The castle will be under attack soon. I must get you and our child to safety."

Larenta shook her head as if to clear it. "What are you saying? How can it be under attack? By whom? Who would dare?"

Everes cupped her cheek. "The cities of Strom and Fairs have fallen. So have the lands to the south and east. There are creatures unlike any we have seen."

Larenta stared at him in confusion. "Our magic—"

Everes shook his head. "There are too many. My heart, you must take our daughter and seek shelter to the north."

Screams rent the air, and Wynter jumped. She walked over to the doors leading to a balcony and stepped out. Inhabitants not fast enough to reach the stone walls surrounding the castle fell under a black hoard of advancing forces. Wynter lifted her fist to her mouth when she saw a red beam of light turning people to ash.

She turned when Larenta stepped out beside her. Anguish twisted the woman's beautiful features. She swayed again and the man wrapped his arm around her waist.

"I must stop them. I must protect our people."

"No, my love, you are weak from giving birth, and there are too many. It would destroy you!"

Tears coursed down Larenta's cheeks. "They cannot breach the walls, Everes. You know that. If they take Erindale Castle, there is no distance we can run and be safe. We are the stronghold. Erindale is the birthplace of our magic. I must... do what I can. You must call the protectors to the walls."

Everes stiffened and paled. Finally, he whispered, "I will love you for all eternity, my beautiful Queen." He caressed Larenta's cheek before tenderly kissing her.

Everes walked over to the cradle. When he brushed his knuckles tenderly along the babe's cheek, Wynter touched her own cheek, gasping when she felt the King's caress.

"My beautiful daughter. You will one day return and free our people."

This time a tear did escape and course down his cheek. He kissed the infant's cheek before he turned with a tortured expression. As he exited the room, he gave a low order to the Queen's attendants to follow him. Wynter kept her fingers pressed to her cheek, sure that she had felt the touch of warm lips against her skin.

She returned to the balcony. The swarm of invaders were almost to the wall surrounding the castle and interior city. A few minutes later, she could see Everes and eleven other men climbing to a series of platforms on the high wall.

Larenta drew a sobbing breath and murmured, "I love you, my King."

The group on the wall raised their staffs. Everes turned and looked up at Larenta before he slammed his staff down with both hands.

Larenta began to speak in a language that washed through Wynter. It was the language she spoke in her head when she used her powers. The ancient power coursing through her grew in strength and she understood perfectly what her mother chanted.

*"I command the powers of the ancients to give me their strength. Light of my light. Blood of my blood. I command the power of the stars, the planets, and the spirits of my people. I will defend you to my last breath. Protect my land. Protect my people. Banish the creatures to the bowels of the earth. Set the protectors upon these walls and let none breach their defenses. I so command it!"* Larenta lifted her arms and spread her hands.

White lightning and blue streaks flashed from Larenta's body. The blue bolts hit Everes first before arcing horizontally and connecting with each of the men standing on the platforms. White and blue light rolled down the face of the ramparts.

The flow of energy looked like a tsunami, growing larger until it crashed down on the dark, horrific creatures. The ground under the creatures' feet heaved and split, ripping open a crevice that spread as far as the eye could see. Hoards of the creatures fell into the widening gap. Yet even as she watched, others used their peers as stepping stones to make it out of the crevice.

A low moaning cry slipped from Larenta and her knees buckled. Wynter wrapped her arms around her mother. Shock held her immobile when their bodies connected and she held her mother upright. Her energy flowed into her mother, surging until it crashed down on the creatures. More creatures came however, those that survived the magic defenses still pouring forward, undeterred.

"I can do no more," Larenta whispered in a drained voice.

"You must lie down," Wynter urged, guiding Larenta back into the bedroom.

Tears blinded her as her mother paused by the cradle to lift her newborn babe into her arms. Larenta climbed onto the bed, rocking the babe and cooing softly to her. Tortured sobs filled the room as Larenta rocked back and forth, her body shaking.

"Pow-pow, we have to do something," Wynter cried.

Pow-pow shook his head. "These are memories, Wynter. What has happened cannot be changed."

Tears coursed down Wynter's cheeks as the creatures' thunderous rampage overwhelmed the last of their magic defenses and they breached the walls. In that moment of despair, Wynter turned and saw Arastan through the window of the Ring of Power. Larenta twisted toward the glowing circle. Wynter's breath caught in her throat as Larenta begged the man who would become her father to take and protect her child. When Arastan nodded, she sent Wynter through the doorway between their worlds—magic to magic, one loving, devoted parent to another.

The door to the bedchamber burst open and one of the alien creatures stepped in. Pow-pow drew Wynter close and Larenta released the last of her magic just as the creature fired its weapon at her. The two powers combined in an explosive force that rippled through the kingdom, turning the alien creatures to ash and Larenta's people to stone.

Wynter pushed on Pow-pow's front legs until he released her. She walked over to the bed. Tears streamed down her cheeks as she lifted her hands and whispered an ancient spell.

"Sleep i uireb sleep -o mín núr. Glenn- bar na i galad where mín came a rad- sídh, nin rís. Nin naneth." *Sleep the eternal sleep of our people. Go home to the light from whence we came and find peace, my Queen... my mother.*

The soft, powdery flakes that made up Larenta's body transformed into brilliant prisms of tiny lights that rose from the bed. Wynter followed them when they floated out of the balcony's French doors. They rose higher and higher until she couldn't see them anymore.

"Pow-pow, take me for a ride. I want to see my parents' home," she quietly requested.

"It would be my honor, Princess Wynter of Erindale," Pow-pow said with a sad smile as he bowed his head.

# Chapter Seven

Pow-pow flew over the sun-drenched land. The castle seemed frozen in time. Stone residents remained forever captured in their last moment. Twelve protectors stood as sentinels over the kingdom. White energy and royal blue lightning crackled between them.

Outside the castle walls, a long ravine stretched for nearly a mile in each direction. The gap was so deep that at one time molten rock from the planet's core had flowed within it, leaving a hard crust as evidence. On the other side of the ravine was a blackened forest. Ghostly trunks of dead trees populated the landscape for hundreds of yards into the once lush forest.

Past the dead trees, life thrived. Wynter saw a frightened herd of deer running through a meadow and a pack of wolves that sought cover in the thick forest as Pow-pow's shadow passed over them. A lone bear ambled along the riverbank, undisturbed by the dragon flying overhead.

Wynter tucked her head close to Pow-pow's scales as she thought of her biological parents. It was painful to think about their lives being cut short by the strange creatures. It also hurt to think about her adoptive parents. Why had they kept the truth from her? Why did her father hide this ring? Did he plan to tell her about her birthplace someday or would he have kept it a secret forever?

A spiral of smoke rose through the trees nearly fifty miles from the castle. Wynter's breath caught when she saw a girl of about thirteen carrying a basket to a quaint hut surrounded by six outbuildings and several pens filled with livestock. The girl looked up and froze.

At Wynter's silent request, Pow-pow circled overhead. She knew her parents' creed. She should never interfere and she should never allow knowledge or suspicion of the Mage-line—but how could such a thing be wrong when she belonged here?

The girl dropped her woven basket and ran for the hut, screaming. The door swung open and a woman in her mid-thirties caught and held the girl against her body, searching the area nearby before looking up and noticing their presence with alarm. The woman pulled the girl inside and slammed the door.

"Land, Pow-pow," she requested.

The powerful stone dragon circled around again before landing lightly on the uneven, grassy turf. Wynter swung her leg over Pow-pow's broad shoulders and slid off, her boots sinking into the soft soil. She picked up the contents of the girl's basket from the ground and placed them back inside. When a man of similar age to the woman stepped out of the hut, his sword braced for an attack, she straightened. The woman stood in the doorway behind him, the young girl peeking out from behind her.

"Hello," Wynter hesitantly called. "Your... daughter dropped her basket. I'm sorry we startled her."

She stepped forward, holding out the basket. The couple stared at her with wide eyes. She took another step forward.

Pale and tense, the man looked from her face, to Pow-pow, to the basket, and back again. He tentatively approached her, and the longer he looked at her face, the more he seemed to be having trouble catching his breath.

"Can you... can you understand me?" she asked, biting her lip.

"Yes, Your Highness. I am Tomas," the man said, his voice barely above a whisper.

Wynter tried to smile. She waved to Pow-pow and forced out a laugh.

"That's Pow-pow. He's harmless." She ignored Pow-pow's humph of disagreement. "My name is Wynter."

"Yes, Your Highness," Tomas choked out, lowering to his knee and bowing his head.

"You... you know who I am?" she asked, glancing at the woman who was curtsying deeply.

"You are the lost Princess of Erindale, thought murdered with your parents when the creatures attacked," Tomas said.

His voice trembled, and he glanced up at her before bowing his head again. Wynter placed the basket on the ground next to him and reached for his hand. Tomas shuddered when she touched him.

"Please... can you tell me what happened?"

Tomas nodded and together they stood. The woman gave her a tentative smile before stepping back. The little girl ran over and collected the basket.

"I'm Desiree," the little girl introduced with a curtsy.

"I'm Wynter and this is Pow-pow. He's a stone dragon."

"Welcome to our home. I'm LaNie, Your Highness," the woman introduced with another deep curtsy.

Wynter paused in the doorway and looked back at Pow-pow. He was lying in the yard, gnawing on a rock, while half a dozen chickens pecked around him. He motioned with his head for her to go.

*I will be here if you need me,* he promised.

She gave a slight nod before taking a deep breath. She was nervous and sad, but she was also exhilarated. This was finally a chance to find out who she really was and where she belonged in this vast, crazy universe.

———

Two hours later, Wynter emerged from the house, pale but composed. She knew Pow-pow's sharp hearing had easily followed along with the conversation, so there wasn't any point in her repeating what was said.

Tomas and LaNie didn't know where the creatures came from. They only knew of the massive destruction left behind. The creatures were too fast to out-run, but Tomas and LaNie specialized in magic that hid them from threats.

They had lived in a village far to the south of Erindale when the first attacks began, and they traveled farther and farther north to find land that had recovered from the blight the invaders brought. Erindale was situated above a strong source of magic, and so it was here, just outside the blast zone of the castle, that the land first began to flourish.

"Go home now?" Pow-pow asked, rising to his feet and stretching.

Wynter shook her head. "No, I'm… not ready. Not yet. I… need someplace where I can think," she quietly replied, petting his neck.

"Pick a place," he suggested.

Wynter's fingers went to the ring she always wore around her neck.

"There is a place I would like to visit again," she said, looking up at Pow-pow.

"Does it have rocks?" Pow-pow asked.

"Yes, and lots and lots of sand," she laughingly replied with a rueful shake of her head.

---

**Earth:**

Khalid nodded to the guards in the corridor. Adham grimly approached from the opposite direction.

"You haven't found my uncle?" Khalid asked.

Adham shook his head. "No. I've ordered a second search of every room in the palace."

Khalid sighed. "He may try to escape over the border. Notify the other commanders."

"Already done."

"Good. Sooner or later, he will be found."

"You should let one of the medics check you out. That wound in your side—"

Khalid waved a hand in dismissal. "It is just a graze. I'll be fine."

Khalid moved to pass him and Adham touched his arm. He shot the older man an impatient glare. The compassion in Adham's eyes made him look away.

"I'm fine, Adham. I… need a moment alone."

"Be careful. You can't let your guard down until your uncle is caught and we have contained the resistance."

"You've trained me well, Adham. I will be attentive," he promised. Even so, he knew there would be two guards hovering just out of sight in case there was trouble. That was protocol, and so was informing a separate guard of his intended location. "I will be in my mother's garden," he said.

Adham dipped his head. "May you find peace, my King."

Khalid shuddered as Adham walked away but quickly shook off the reaction to his father's title and turned the corner. The corridor ended at a set of massive wooden doors. He pushed them open.

As he slowly walked through his mother's private library, he noted that the beautiful room had not changed very much.

*At least my uncle did one thing right,* he thought.

There were rumors that his uncle Inarus had a jealous, possessive love for his mother. Poisoning her had been her punishment for not returning his affection. When she got well, Inarus often stated it was destiny keeping her alive, so he instead focused on killing the King and his heir.

On the day of their demise, Queen Faiza wasn't supposed to be in the same car as the King. Khalid and his father were supposed to travel together while his mother waited at their destination.

The death of Faiza had sent Inarus spiraling into full-blown insanity, and the people of Aethon had paid dearly for it—especially when they refused to turn over the young prince. Khalid cursed, wanting to keep all the memories locked in the dark recesses of his mind.

He exited through the double doors, pausing on the patio to look at the neglected garden in the moonlight. Sinking down onto the steps, he took deep breaths, bowed his head, and closed his eyes. His pounding heart set a frantic pace for the memories crowding his mind; memories of his parents, the citizens who had rallied against a tyrant, and the dead who would never see their triumph.

He was so lost in the past that he dismissed the first soft caress against his cheek as the wind. It wasn't until he felt the brush of softness again, this time on his right cheek, that he lashed out and gripped the soft petals of a rose in a tight hold.

Surprise held him immobile when the soft curves of a woman suddenly materialized in front of him like an apparition coming to life. A long, dark brown overcoat partially covered her matching vest. Her royal blue shirt revealed a shadow of cleavage. Dark brown tweed pants and knee-high riding boots encased her coltish legs. She knelt, and he found himself staring into the same vivid, emerald eyes that had haunted him for more than half his life.

"Khalid."

The lilting voice from his past had matured. Her mane of platinum hair was pulled back from her face, contained in a long plait down her back. He mentally calculated her age and bit back a groan. She would be around seventeen or eighteen. He was a man of twenty-eight and should absolutely not be feeling what he was feeling.

His two guards gave harsh cries of warning and moved to protect their king from the intruder that had suddenly appeared in front of him. Khalid raised his hand, his fist tight, to let them know he was safe.

"Leave us," he ordered without looking around.

Khalid looked at the rose in Wynter's hand. The damage he had done to it was repairing before his eyes. Wynter smiled and brushed his cheek with it again before offering it to him. He absently accepted the uncrushed bloom.

"Wynter," he murmured.

Concern darkened her eyes. She touched his temple where exploding glass had cut it. He stiffened, and warmth spread through him, taking his breath away.

"Ancient energui tul- na nin a on- nin i rod plural rodyn na heal hin wounds," she chanted.

The words were like music that calmed and healed. He wanted to touch her but was afraid to move. The warmth was spreading down his body, and he swore he could feel his torn flesh mending.

Seconds lengthened to a minute, then two, before she sat back with a satisfied expression. The numerous small wounds all over his body no longer caused him discomfort.

A long strand of her hair had come loose from her plait. When he tucked it behind her ear, electricity sizzled against his fingertips. It wasn't unpleasant, but there was definitely a charge.

"Where have you been? Where did you go? Why are you here?" he asked, his frustration growing with each question.

She tilted her head, a questioning expression on her face, and covered his hand with hers, shaking her head. Then she rose and looked into the garden as if something had drawn her attention. Khalid rose as well but he didn't see or hear anything. He captured her wrist and she startled. He had to force himself to loosen his grip so he didn't bruise her.

The top of her head almost reached his chin. She turned to him and lifted her free hand to his temple, pressing two fingers against his skin as if she were trying to read his mind. She closed her eyes, and her lips moved silently.

When she opened her eyes to meet his, she said, "I came here searching for... peace."

Khalid stepped back in surprise, releasing her wrist. She had spoken in perfect Arabic! The newfound way to connect with her made him ache to connect in other ways. He wanted to wrap her hair around his fist and pull her against him. He wanted.... With a shake of his head to clear it, he focused on her words.

"Your mother... sang in this garden, and... it was magic that was not magic. It made me feel."

It had been such a long time since Khalid had heard his mother sing. He had so many memories associated with her beautiful voice.

"Is she not well?" Wynter asked with concern.

"She's... dead. I couldn't keep her safe," he said, his voice thick with emotion.

"I... am so sorry. My mother... also," she replied with a haunted expression.

Her eyes filled with tears, and she tipped her head forward, burying her face against his chest. She wrapped her arms around his waist, and he held her as she sniffled.

"I'm sorry for your loss," he murmured. "My mother— She died a long time ago."

Her breath came out as a hiccup, and she nodded. He caressed her back, his mind reeling from her return and his body heating from having her in his arms. He had so many questions.

"Why did you return? Where... who are you and where did you go? How can you speak my language now?"

She pulled away from him, and panic seized him she would suddenly disappear again. He held onto her hand, preventing her from moving too far. She squeezed his fingers and sank down onto the step, pulling him gently down beside her.

"It is forbidden to interfere with worlds who do not know about us," she said, glancing at him before looking at the overgrown garden. She seemed to have become fully fluent in his language in just seconds! And what she was saying... it was incredible.

"Who are you?" he repeated.

She lifted a slender shoulder. "I... don't know anymore. I was raised among the Mages of Enyo. My mother and father are researchers. My father developed the Rings of Power. They open windows to other worlds, facilitating observation without interference. My mother studies the fauna and flora of the different worlds. She has discovered new medicines that have helped many worlds. We live on Zelos. The natives know about mages and other off-worlders."

"Wait.... Are you saying— Are you saying... *aliens* exist?" he choked out, releasing her hand and shifting slightly away.

She smiled slightly. "Of course. Do you really think there are all those universes out there," she said with a wave toward the stars, "but no species can exist anywhere but here?"

Khalid's gaze automatically followed her hand. Brilliant stars glittered above them despite the full moon. The power grid was still down. A team would be working on repairing the damage left by his uncle's retreating forces.

"Where is Enyo?" he asked, searching the sky.

Wynter's delighted laughter and mischievous expression made him smile. He needed to touch her again, and he casually moved his hand toward where hers rested on the step. "You cannot see it from here. It is—"

He touched her hand, stroking her soft skin.

"...a very long way away," she said, her voice softening.

"Mages... are witches," he said with a frown.

"Of sorts. Mages use technology along with magic," she said.

"So, you are a mage?"

She nodded. "Yes, and... more. What happened to you? You were hurt."

"After you disappeared, things became better for a while, but there were still attacks." He explained as briefly as he could about his uncle before finishing with what had happened in the last few weeks. "There has been a ground-swell of rebellion against my uncle. My supporters and I rooted him out of the palace tonight, but he is not in our custody. He got away."

She threaded her fingers through his and gently squeezed them. "War is never good, but sometimes it is necessary. I wish I could have protected your parents."

A desire to hold her and never let her go surged through him, as ancient and primitive as time. Deep down, he knew she belonged to him—and that he belonged to her. He didn't understand it and didn't even bother trying. Her very existence was just as incredible as his certainty of the love they would share, and it didn't matter how strange any of this was. She was here, and he felt what he felt.

A low growl, unearthly and dangerous reached his ears. The hair on the back of his neck rose, and he pulled Wynter behind him as he reached for his weapon. His two guards appeared from the shadows again, their weapons drawn.

The menacing rumble came again, and the men nervously closed ranks when the ground vibrated under their feet. Khalid's gaze scanned the area, searching for the danger.

"Third-floor balcony on your right. There is a man there with a weapon," Wynter warned.

Wynter stepped in front of him and lifted her arms just as a massive black shadow exploded from the garden toward the upper-level balcony and gunfire erupted. In seconds, the only sound was a terrified scream and crunching bones.

Khalid and his guards opened fire on the creature that was eating the attacker on the third balcony.

"Do not use your weapons!" Wynter cried.

"Follow her orders," Khalid hoarsely relayed to his men, reluctantly forcing himself to move his own finger away from the trigger of his gun.

*The 'amirat khurafiat alsahra must know what she's doing*, he thought with extreme apprehension.

The creature turned glowing green eyes toward them and spit the man out. The body landed with a heavy thud in the garden.

Farid and Mousa were praying in low, terrified voices, their eyes wide. More soldiers entered the garden, drawn by the sound of the gunfire.

"Do not fire!" Khalid ordered the newcomers, breathing deeply as he continued to trust Wynter's judgement in the face of a giant man-eater unlike any he had ever seen. Khalid distantly felt Wynter pushing his weapon down so he was no longer aiming at the creature.

The monster released a heated snort before climbing the wall to the roof. In a burst of speed that almost knocked everyone over, the creature unfurled massive wings and took off into the night sky.

"Was that…. Was that a dragon?" he faintly inquired.

Wynter's eyes widened as the once quiet garden filled with men. She took a stumbling step down the steps, her heart pounding as the weight of what she had done dawned on her.

# Chapter Eight

Khalid stared at the mangled remains of his uncle. There were deep slashes the size of dinner plates in his body. His head had been found several feet away. His automatic rifle was bent in half.

Where the creature had climbed, there were deep gouges in the marble wall. Mousa and Farid stood with Wynter between them, their eyes nervously moving from her to the rooftop and back again. She was watching him with a haunted expression.

"Adham, please dispose of Inarus's remains," he requested.

"What happened, Khalid? This... what could do this?" Adham demanded, his voice tense with nervousness.

Khalid couldn't keep his eyes off Wynter. "You wouldn't believe me if I told you," he replied.

Adham reached toward Khalid, studying his face. "Your wounds are healed."

"Yes," Khalid said, not expanding on the subject.

Adham's gaze moved to Wynter. "The woman... who is she?"

"No one you should be concerned about," Khalid answered.

"I would like to speak with her," Adham stated.

"No!" The denial burst out of Khalid with such vehemence that it surprised the men standing around him.

Adham looked thoughtfully between Wynter and his king. He could see the wariness in his friend's eyes. Khalid rested his hand on Adham's arm.

"She is not a threat to me, Adham. She… is an old friend."

"Where did she come from? What was she doing in the palace? Khalid, you don't know if she supported your uncle. Even though he is dead now, that doesn't mean she might not have an agenda of her own."

Khalid smiled and shook his head. "She has nothing to do with my uncle. You'll have to trust me on this, Adham. I… promised her long ago that I would always protect her. She means me no harm."

Adham didn't look convinced, but he bowed his head. With a sharp order, Adham instructed two men carrying body bags to remove Inarus's remains.

Wynter closed her eyes and turned her head away from the gruesome scene. Khalid walked over and gently cupped her elbow.

"Come, let's go inside," he said.

She nodded, a shudder running through her as the men performed the grisly task. Khalid didn't miss the way she glanced up at the sky before they entered the palace. He looked up as well but saw nothing.

"Where is it?" he asked.

She bit her lip as they climbed the steps. "He's flying overhead, keeping an eye on me."

He guided her to a seat in his mother's library. She looked pale in the dim light the emergency generators provided.

"Would you like something to drink?" he asked.

She shook her head. Her eyes moved to the gardens outside the French doors. She looked sad and worried, but most of all, she looked fragile.

"I should leave as soon as the garden is clear of people," she murmured. "It was wrong of me to come here."

"No! You left once. I won't let you go again," he growled.

"You have no choice. I don't belong here," she quietly responded.

---

Wynter's stomach churned with stress. She had broken the most crucial rule of the Mage-line order. Worse, she had betrayed her parents' trust.

Khalid had reacted to Pow-pow with horror and intense fear. This world was not at all like Erindale, a place that was probably not used to dragons but had already been visited by aliens, already used magic, and was... sort-of a home for Wynter. She was born there, and in some ways, she belonged there—and Pow-pow belonged wherever she belonged. Khalid's world, however, was not accustomed to creatures such as herself and Pow-pow.

Fear for her friend poured through her. Pow-pow assured her that the humans' weapons could not hurt him. The worst thing that could happen to him was being forced to chomp down on more humans.

*They squishy and taste terrible,* Pow-pow said, trying to spit out the horrid, metallic flavor.

Wynter returned her attention to Khalid, who was pacing in agitation. He kept glancing at the garden in nervous apprehension until he abruptly twisted around and faced her.

"You do belong here—with me," Khalid declared.

He looked wild, confused, and fierce. His expression reminded her so much of when they were younger.

She rose from her seat and walked over to him. He had become a strikingly handsome man with strong features. She touched his neatly trimmed beard. The coarse black hair was surprisingly pleasant under her fingertips. His jaw was clenched, and his lips pressed together. His defiant eyes had darkened until they appeared almost as black as his hair.

She stroked the long silky strands of hair near his ear that his headdress didn't hide. Time seemed to slow as she studied him.

Why did she feel such a connection to him? Her young heart beat heavily at the idea of leaving him, but what choice did she have? She and Pow-pow could not remain on this world. She knew from her father's notes and illustrations that she and Pow-pow would be in danger themselves, but they would also imperil anyone who associated with them.

Memories of the world she was born in flashed through her mind. The devastation left by the hoard of aliens still affected the survivors nearly two decades later. While she and Pow-pow would never intentionally harm another, there could still be long-term damaging effects if they stayed here.

"Don't leave me." Khalid slid his hand against her nape and tugged her closer. She gasped when he captured her lips.

Wynter had never been kissed before. The sensation startled and intrigued her. Her lips parted under the pressure of his, and he swept his tongue inside. Her eyes fluttered closed as a pulsing need spread through her.

*This is right,* she thought.

Her heart hammered against her chest, and her hands pressed over his pounding heart. Blood swooshed in her ears. All she could hear or feel was him. She wrapped her arms around his neck and pressed her body closer to his in utter abandon.

*Two hearts, one heartbeat. As if two halves of a soul have found each other across the universe… and become one.*

The next afternoon, Khalid strode down the corridor that led to his living quarters. They were his rooms when he originally lived here. Already, work was underway to repair the palace and the country. It would take years, but resources, manpower, and hope were powerful driving forces.

*Hope,* he thought.

His thoughts should have been on his early morning meeting with Adham and his other military advisors. He should have been thinking about the many meetings that would fill the next few weeks as the new government was established and his place as Ruler of Aethon was sealed. There were a million and one things to think about that didn't involve a platinum-blonde woman from another world.

*Don't forget her dragon!* he reminded himself with a slight shudder.

Khalid shook his head at the thought. After he kissed her last night….

*I don't care if she has a hundred dragons, trolls, fairies, or other mythical creatures. She is mine.*

That knowledge gave him hope. He believed their destinies were written years ago when Wynter first appeared, and their intense chemistry yesterday was yet another sign that they were meant for each other. If Adham hadn't interrupted them, he suspected she would have fully belonged to him.

"Your Highness."

Khalid groaned when he heard Colonel Giaffar Gindibuh call out to him. He wanted to ignore his friend. He was exhausted and more than a little impatient to see Wynter. Breathing deeply, he slowed his pace, allowing Giaffar to catch up with him.

"What is it, Giaf?" he wearily inquired.

Giaffar was the same age as he was. The son of a Boeheim sheikh, they were childhood friends. Giaf had planned and fought beside him every step of the way over the last ten years.

"Is it true? About the girl," Giaf asked.

"Is it true there is a *woman* here in the palace, in my quarters, then yes," he replied in a short tone.

Giaf eyed him with a steady stare that made his cheeks darken. Thanks to the events in his life, romantic relationships had been limited to a few awkward kisses and a lot of wishful thinking. Giaf had a slightly more expansive experience but not by much.

"Who is she? Adham is tightlipped. Some guards have been saying—"

Khalid stopped and faced his friend with a scowl. "What have the guards been saying?" he demanded.

This time it was Giaf who flushed. Giaf's face was tense and his shoulders stiff. Uncertainty flashed through his eyes.

"I saw the marks in the wall and read the report of Inarus's death. Farid and Mousa swear they saw a... dragon. Doctor Baqir's medical report states Inarus suffered multiple lacerations that went completely through his body, and that his head was ripped off, his skull crushed," Giaf warily replied.

Khalid stood frozen for a moment before briefly closing his eyes.

"I want all reports of what happened to my uncle contained," he ordered.

Giaf uttered a low curse and gripped his arm. "Are you telling me what Farid and Mousa reported was true? That there was a dragon... and the girl speaks to it?"

Khalid pursed his lips and looked over Giaf's shoulder to where his other two personal guards, Hagar and Habanamru, stood in silence. He knew now that Farid and Mousa would probably have already briefed them about what they saw in the courtyard.

"Who else knows about this?" he asked as he wearily rubbed the back of his neck.

Giaf paled when he didn't deny the claim. "Adham, me, your guards, and I think Doctor Baqir suspects. There are others that were in the courtyard and saw the gouges in the wall," he answered.

"I… will brief you, Adham, Doctor Baqir, and my guards in one hour in the conference room. Until then, I ask that you make sure that nothing else is said."

Giaf nodded in agreement. "I'll let the others know." He glanced down the corridor. "And the girl… woman? What about her?"

Khalid gazed at the double doors at the end of the corridor. Behind those doors was the most precious thing in his life. He would do whatever he must to protect her.

"She is mine, Giaf. That is all you need to know," he said before turning and walking away.

At the end of the corridor, he opened the door to his living quarters with a murmur to Habanamru and Hagar to remain outside. Both guards cast a wary look at each other and then at him before reluctantly nodding. He stepped through the door, closing it quietly behind him.

He froze, taking in the sight of Wynter's bemused face as she listened to Dhat-Badan. He had requested the Wise Woman's presence. He knew she would want to see Wynter again, and the moment she discovered that the strange child had returned, she had eagerly agreed to come.

"Pow-pow only eats dirt, rocks, and such? How can he live on such things?" Dhat-Badan was asking.

"He's a rock dragon. Why would he want to eat anything else?"

"Are there other types of dragons?" Dhat-Badan asked.

"Oh, yes. There are many others," Wynter replied.

Dhat-Badan finished braiding Wynter's hair before looking up and smiling at Khalid. Wynter turned, her eyes widening at the sight of him, and a faint pink color rushed to her cheeks. Her eyes skimmed his face before settling on his lips. Khalid's body immediately reacted to the darkening green in her eyes.

"It is wonderful to see you, Dhat-Badan. We would be pleased to have your company again tomorrow," he said.

"It has been a pleasure, Your Highness," Dhat-Badan acknowledged with a bow of her head.

Khalid stepped away from the door as Dhat-Badan passed him and exited the room. He stood still, drinking in the glow of Wynter's beauty and the fact that she was real.

"You're still here," he said.

He cleared his throat when the words came out with a slight croak. She laughed and stood up. The movement was graceful, like a ballerina. She was dressed in one of Aethon's traditional robes.

"Yes. Dhat-Badan has been telling me about the major events of the past few years," she said.

He met her halfway across the room, enveloping her in his arms and capturing her upturned lips. It had been practically impossible for him to think of anything but holding and kissing her again. She returned his kiss, opening for him like a desert blossom receiving its first rainfall.

Heart pounding, his body aroused in a way he had never experienced before, he wanted to touch her all over. He slid his hands up her body and captured her face, tilting her head so he could kiss her deeper. She slid her hands down his arms to his wrists and broke their kiss to gaze up at him with a look of wonder and confusion.

"What is it, Khalid?" she asked, tenderly caressing his brow as he breathed heavily.

He rested his forehead against hers and sighed. "Nothing is wrong. I just missed you," he said.

Her expression softened, and she leaned forward, kissing him again. This kiss was soft... gentle. She chanted words he didn't understand, and the tension headache that had been throbbing with a dull ache faded.

"You need time to clean up, eat, and rest," she gently reproached.

"I need you," he replied.

# Chapter Nine

Wynter's heart melted at the slightly vulnerable note in Khalid's voice. Warmth filled her and a powerful emotion surged inside her. She was falling in love with Khalid.

His touch awakened the power inside her, touching her on a level she had never experienced before. Tiny charges of electricity swept through her when they touched, and his unique scent—sandalwood, spice, and the fragrance of the desert—made her want to crawl all over him.

Even tired and disheveled, she wanted him. She entwined her fingers with his and guided him toward his bedroom.

She could have used a spell to remove his clothing, but there was a unique intimacy in undressing him. She kept her eyes on his face as she began unwrapping his robe. It fell to the floor and revealed a long-sleeved linen shirt that buttoned down the front.

His breathing increased as she undid each button, kissing his heated flesh as it was exposed. She dropped the shirt onto his discarded robe. Her lips parted in wonder as she lightly caressed his shoulders and ribcage.

She brushed the light matting of hair on his chest with her lips and stopped at his taut nipple. Unable to resist, she flicked it with her tongue.

"By the sands of the desert, Wynter, you don't know what you are doing to me," he groaned, his head falling forward and his face stiff with need.

"I do, because you do the same thing to me," she murmured.

She undid the button of his trousers, and they fell to the floor around his ankles. With a wave of her hand, his clothing disappeared along with hers. They reappeared on a nearby chair. She was growing impatient for him.

The sound of Khalid's groan filled the room. He could no longer hold himself back. He had to touch her. Wynter reveled in the sensation of his rough hands against her soft skin. She grasped his hand and pulled him into the bathroom.

The water in the shower automatically turned on as they stepped into it. Cold water turned warm as she wrapped one hand around Khalid's neck, pulling his head down to her, and gripping his throbbing cock with the other.

"I need you, too, Khalid," she whispered against his lips.

Wynter had never been so sure of anything in her life. She caressed Khalid's wet flesh, memorizing every inch of him.

She didn't know how long they could be together. If she had her way, it would be forever—yet, she also knew that would be impossible.

"Wynter," Khalid groaned.

He cupped her breasts and locked onto one of her taut nipples with his lips while pinching the other between his index finger and thumb. Her hips jerked forward in response, her breath coming in pants as the fire of need ripped through her body and settled like molten lava between her legs.

She rocked her hips in an instinctive dance, desperation flooding her body. His hand slid between her legs, and she shifted her grip to his shoulders as he caressed her.

"Please, Khalid," she moaned.

Khalid cursed and straightened. He quickly soaped down his body before rinsing. Turning off the shower, he grabbed two of the towels. Wynter shook her head and whispered a chant.

Water droplets rose from their bodies, swirling together until they formed a tiny waterspout and splashed down the drain. Khalid's eyes widened, but he didn't say a thing. He stepped out of the shower, scooped her up into his arms, and strode to his bedroom.

He laid her down on the covers before falling over her with a deluge of hungry, passionate kisses that left her trembling with need. She could feel his thick cock pressing against the inside of her leg. She scored his back with her nails, needing him to fill her.

"I have to… I need your… pleasure… first," he gritted out.

She cupped his cheeks, looking up at him with glowing emerald eyes filled with love. His desire for her and his need to ensure her pleasure were gifts that she would always hold dear to her heart. Sliding her hand down between them, she guided his shaft to her ready channel.

"Together, Khalid. We will find our pleasure together," she breathed.

She pulled his head down, kissing him, and wound her legs around his waist, opening her body to him. When he filled her, the exquisite sensation of him filling her—stretching her—sent her over the precipice.

She arched backward, lifting her hips and driving him through the barrier of her virginity, squeezing him as she came. Gasping for breath, she held him as he rocked into her. The flash of pain turned to intense pleasure as Khalid moved.

"Oh, Khalid, I love you," Wynter cried out.

Her body was shattering around her as an intense orgasm washed through her in waves. Khalid held her tighter, and his strokes became harder, deeper, and more frenzied. She watched his face in a haze of passion, his eyes closed, his expression tensing, and his lips parted for a moment before he cried out.

Wynter felt his cock pulsing inside of her, and she tightened her arms around him to keep him locked to her. Her heart swelled when he collapsed, holding her to him as if he would never let her go.

"You must never leave me. I love you, *habibi*," he said in a hoarse voice.

---

An hour and a half later, Khalid shut the door behind him, breathing deeply to keep control of his raging emotions. He was late for the meeting he had scheduled with Giaf, Adham, and his guards. He rested his hand on the door, remembering how beautiful Wynter looked lying in his bed.

"Is everything alright, Your Highness?" Hagar inquired.

Khalid nodded. "Yes, I want to have a meeting with you both," he said.

He turned and strode away from his quarters. His mind whirled while his body hummed with contentment. He could still taste Wynter on his lips. He remembered the sensation of her body wrapped around his, and silently cursed when heat pooled and his cock responded.

Several minutes later, he entered the conference room, followed by Hagar and Habanamru. The other men were already there, seated at a large conference table. He gave them a brief nod before rounding the table and waving Hagar and Habanamru to their seats.

"I know there are questions, and I will answer them the best I can. What is shared in this room will go no further," he stated in a hard voice.

Doctor Baqir peered over his glasses. He was a short, round man dressed in traditional robes. His bald head was covered by a kaffiyeh.

Baqir had been his father's physician and was close to seventy years old.

"I suspect this has something to do with your uncle's death," Doctor Baqir responded curiously.

Khalid nodded, turning his attention to Farid and Mousa, who were sitting in silence. Both men were hesitant to meet his eyes.

"Farid, Mousa, would you like to respond?" he asked.

Mousa glanced at him before shaking his head and staring straight ahead. Farid swallowed. Khalid took pity on the man.

"Say it, Farid," he quietly encouraged.

"Was it really a dragon?" Farid asked.

"Yes."

Khalid breathed a sigh of relief. It was finally out. In a way, this cemented Wynter's presence in his life, and it made the fantastical elements seem more real now that more people had seen them.

Talk erupted around the table. When Khalid was finally able to get a word in edgewise, he told them the whole story, including how Wynter cured the Queen, disappeared into a portal, and recently told him about alien life in many worlds.

Talk exploded around the table again. Khalid gritted his teeth. The words 'monsters' and 'invasion' filtered through.

"It is *not* an invasion! It is one person," he growled.

"And a dragon," Habanamru grumbled.

Khalid shot the huge, normally silent guard a heated glare. "And a dragon," he conceded.

"What happened in the courtyard?" Giaf asked.

"My uncle opened fire on us. Wynter protected us from the bullets, and the dragon climbed the wall and took care of Inarus," he replied.

"A dragon would explain the wounds to your uncle's body," Doctor Baqir murmured with a satisfied expression.

Giaf shook his head. "So, what… how… do we handle an alien woman and her pet dragon?" he asked.

Silence fell around the table. It was the first time any of them had really thought about the logistics of dealing with such an extraordinary situation. This was far different from overthrowing a tyrant. The rest of the world could look the other way when it came to toppling an abusive regime. Aliens and dragons were going to be a little more difficult to explain.

Eventually, Khalid looked at each man with a resolute expression and replied, "Keep her… them… safe. We are going to keep them safe."

# Chapter Ten

The sun was setting on the horizon by the time he dragged himself away. There had been one minor crisis after another. It hadn't helped that his mind had been on Wynter.

He rushed into his living quarters, scanning the area for her with a small amount of desperation. Dhat-Badan looked up from where she was setting a glass of water in the sink with an amused expression. She gave a slight jerk of her head toward the hallway.

"If it helps, she has missed you, too, Your Highness. I will retire for the night now," Dhat-Badan said.

"Yes… thank you. I wish you a good night, Wise Woman."

He didn't hear Dhat-Badan leave. His focus was on Wynter. He entered his bedroom and glanced around. A breeze fluttered the curtains, and he saw her standing on the balcony overlooking the private courtyard.

He joined her. She turned her head and smiled at him. Without thinking, he opened his arms to her, and she flowed into them. Peace flooded him the moment she was in his arms.

*This feels right,* he thought.

He bowed his head and captured her lips. She urgently buried her hands in his hair. His groan mixed with hers. He wanted her to do that magic-thing she did to make all their clothes disappear.

"I want you," he said, peppering her jaw with kisses.

Her breathless laugh drove him wild. He fumbled with her robes, trying to remove them. Her own hands were busy working on his clothes.

"One of these days we will take it slow, I promise."

She laughed again. The sound of her happiness warmed his soul as he scooped her up and carried her to his bedroom.

---

Several hours later, replete from lovemaking, stomach full from their meal, and wrapped comfortably in each other's arms, they stood on the balcony once more. The stars were brilliant in the night sky. Power was still intermittent in the city. Khalid wondered if perhaps a change in the lighting might be wise, so his people could see the stars that had guided their ancestors for centuries. They had guided him.

"What about there? Is there any life in that part of the sky?" he asked, pointing toward the west.

Wynter tilted her head and thought before she nodded. "Yes, Isotope. The Glacians live there. It is a frozen world, but it thrives with life. The people there can control ice. Technically, I shouldn't be telling you this. Worlds that have not mastered space travel should not be… visited. But, I know for a fact that they have violated their own rules."

"What do you mean by that?"

Wynter shook her head. "Perhaps I can tell you one day. I think it best to not tell you too much yet. I wish you could talk to Father. He knows all about each of the worlds and how the multiverse works."

"Multiverse?" he repeated.

"Worlds are layered within each other. Think of it as an onion. You have one onion with many separate layers, but they are still part of that one onion. In this case, it is your world but layered so that it has many levels that exist on their own, yet are still connected. The concept can be... quite headache-inducing," she confessed.

Khalid shook his head. *Humans really aren't ready for these concepts,* he realized.

A shadow passed overhead, and he looked up at the sky. The only way he knew something was there was because of the blackness blocking the stars. He followed the movement and realized that it was Wynter's dragon.

"Will you trust me?" she asked, turning to him with a smile.

He frowned and nodded. "Of course I'll trust you."

She pulled out of his arms, grasped his hand, and pulled him closer to the railing. His eyes widened when she lifted the hem of her robe, climbed up onto the railing, and stood on its narrow surface.

"Follow me," she said.

"Anywhere."

He climbed up beside her, and held onto her waist as they stood on the edge. His breath caught when she twisted and jumped off, pulling him with her. Their plunge to the ground nearly twenty feet below never happened. Instead, they fell only a couple of feet before landing on something hard and smooth.

"Hang on to me," she instructed with a laugh.

*Fly, Pow-pow!*

"Can I talk in front of him, or am I supposed to keep my thoughts to myself?" Pow-pow dryly inquired.

Khalid stiffened with shock. "It can talk?"

Wynter laughed again. "Yes, *he* can talk. Sometimes he never shuts up," she teased.

"Ha-ha," Pow-pow replied sardonically. "Your planet has lots of yummy rocks and sand—lots and lots of sand," Pow-pow rumbled with pleasure.

"I am glad to hear you are enjoying our beloved… planet." Khalid smiled. He had begun his reply automatically, noticing as he did that he was using the standard reply his parents would give visiting dignitaries. He was amused at the unusual circumstance he was using it in now.

"How can something made of rock fly?" he asked.

Pow-pow's deep, rumbling laughter filled the air. "Magic."

Khalid laughed along with Wynter. He shook his head in wonder as he looked down at the city. Sporadic lights twinkled below. He could see fires burning and almost make out people standing and sitting around them. Pride filled him at the knowledge that despite the hardships, his people were happier than they had been in years.

Pow-pow flew toward the desert. At one point, the dragon flew so high that Khalid couldn't resist the urge to raise his hand and try to touch the stars. Wynter said something, her words lost on the wind. When she pointed downward, he saw the Aethon River.

He wrapped his arms tightly around her waist and clenched his legs around Pow-pow when the dragon tucked his wings and dived. A moment before they hit the water, Pow-pow opened his wings and leveled out. The dragon extended his back legs, trailing them along the surface of the water before he swished his clubbed tail back and forth, sending a wave of water outward.

Wynter gestured behind her. A split second later, horses made of water ran beside them. Enchanted, Khalid extended his arm and touched one of them. His fingers skimmed through the cool liquid before the horse surged forward.

"This is… magical," he breathed.

It was well past midnight when Wynter rolled onto her side and absently stroked Khalid's chest. His robes formed their pallet while hers acted as their blanket. Their body heat and the fire that Pow-pow had created for them kept away the chill of the night.

She caressed his face while he stared up at the stars. There was a slight furrow between his eyes. She rubbed it with her index finger.

"What are you thinking about?" she asked.

He pulled her closer, caressing her bare hip. She leaned up on an elbow, forcing him to look at her. Lifting an eyebrow, she waited for his response.

"Nothing… everything… you… Pow-pow… how to hide a dragon… what the future will hold," he murmured.

"Mm, I can't answer the 'nothing' or the 'everything'. I know that I love you, Khalid. I want to be with you. Pow-pow is happy here and can hide very well when he needs to. As to the future, only the mage visionaries can see it, and they will be the first to tell you that nothing is set in stone."

"Except stone dragons," Pow-pow's muttered retort from the darkness made them both smile.

Khalid rolled her onto her back and covered her body with his. Love flooded him, taking his breath away as he gazed down at her. She was so beautiful.

"I love you, Wynter."

She met his kiss. He knew she could taste his desperation, but he didn't care. Whatever the future held, he knew he would fight tooth and nail to keep them together.

Several hours later, Khalid was climbing back onto Pow-pow's back. He tightened his hold on Wynter's waist as the huge stone dragon thundered across the ground and lifted off. Cool air rushed against his face. Pow-pow heated his scales, and the warmth wrapped around them.

"This is like having powered seat warmers," he joked.

Wynter grinned. "Dragons are amazing creatures. Their only natural enemies are giant serpents. I found Pow-pow right after I was here the first time. His egg was the only one left in the nest."

"I don't even want to think how large the serpents must be!" he replied.

The dragon shuddered under them. "Serpents very big. Some larger than a full-grown dragon," Pow-pow said.

Khalid was silent. It still amazed him that a dragon could talk—and he could understand him. The thought of such a powerful beast being afraid of something even bigger and badder was humbling.

"We're almost there," Wynter said.

Khalid could see the silhouette of the city ahead. Soon Pow-pow was gliding through the maze of buildings, sweeping over the palace walls, and landing in the private courtyard. Khalid slid off first before reaching up to help Wynter down.

"Thank you, Pow-pow."

The dragon turned his head and nodded. "It was my pleasure, Your Highness."

Wynter stroked Pow-pow's nose. "Conceal yourself, my friend."

Pow-pow snorted and faded from sight. Khalid would have thought the dragon had just vanished if not for the fact he could still feel heat radiating from him. Khalid reached out a tentative hand. His fingers brushed against the mixture of rough and smooth stone scales.

"Amazing," he murmured with a shake of his head.

"Come, you need sleep. You don't get enough."

Khalid held her hand and followed her inside. As tired as he was, he didn't want to sleep. When he slept, the nightmares came—nightmares of losing his parents, losing the men who had fought beside him, and most frightening of all, the nightmare where Wynter disappeared.

# Chapter Eleven

Life settled into a pattern over the next week. Wynter often spent the days overseeing the rebuilding of Acthon's infrastructure with Khalid. When he was in meetings, she explored the city or worked on restoring Queen Faiza's favorite courtyard to its former glory. It was Wynter's favorite courtyard, too, since it was where she and Khalid had met. The garden was just a little neglected—and now there were claw marks in the wall, so… restoring it was a gift for Khalid, but also, it was really her responsibility. Pow-pow thought the gouges made the courtyard more interesting, so *he* wasn't going to be in charge of fixing it.

The nights were her favorite. They flew over the desert on Pow-pow, discovering beautiful oases and ancient ruins hidden deep in the desert that even Khalid wasn't aware of.

Wynter trailed her fingers along the railing leading down to the main floor. Time was running out. She would *have* to go home in the next few days. It was possible that even now her parents suspected something was wrong. If they had tried to contact her and received no answer, would they return from their trip early?

She was so lost in thought that she didn't see Giaf until she ran into him as she rounded the corner. She stumbled backward, blinking up at him when he grabbed her arms to steady her. He jerked back from her as if he had been burned, and then he blushed.

"I'm sorry. I wasn't paying attention," she apologized.

"I…." He stared at her, his cheeks pink.

She tilted her head and studied him. "You are Giaf, yes?" she asked.

"Yes," he replied with a nod.

With amusement, she said, "I don't bite." She laughed. "I'm Wynter."

He stared down at her outstretched hand as if it were a serpent. She held it for a few seconds, wondering if she was doing something wrong. She had seen many people in the city doing this. He finally reached out and shook her hand before quickly dropping it.

"Where's your dragon?" he asked, glancing at the corridor behind her.

Wynter looked back to see what he was looking at before understanding dawned. She laughed again, the sound echoing against the tall ceiling.

"He's in Queen Faiza's courtyard. Would you like to meet him?"

Giaf's expression wavered between terror and awe. She had to remind herself that this was all new to Khalid's confidants. She looped her arm through Giaf's and changed his direction toward the courtyard.

"Come, he would love to meet someone new. He really enjoys sharing our adventures."

She had to practically drag Giaf the last few feet out of the doors and down the steps.

She paused when Giaf stopped and glanced around the garden with a frown. He paled as he scanned the deep gouges on the wall, and she guessed that he was remembering what Pow-pow had done to Khalid's uncle.

"Pow-pow does not like to eat humans," she assured him.

He looked even more horrified, and she grimaced.

*Poor human is shaking,* Pow-pow observed.

"Pow-pow, I would like you to meet Giaf. He is a friend of Khalid's," she said.

Pow-pow materialized and Giaf stumbled back, tripping on the bottom step. The dragon caught Giaf around the waist with his wing, steadying the man before he could suffer a nasty fall. Wynter tutted when she noticed that Giaf stood stiffly.

"Steady now, human," Pow-pow cautioned.

Giaf blinked and his mouth fell open. He stared into Pow-pow's brilliant green eyes. Wynter decided it might be best to leave the two of them alone to become acquainted without her.

She focused on healing the plants. In the background, she could hear Giaf and Pow-pow talking. Pride, love, and satisfaction swept through her when they laughed.

"You've worked another miracle, I see," Khalid said.

Wynter rose to her feet and twirled when she heard Khalid speak behind her. Before she could say anything, he pulled her into his arms and kissed her. She groaned, wanting to bury her hands in his hair, but refraining when she remembered they were dirty.

"You don't fight fair," she moaned when he gave her a chance to breathe.

"Never, especially when it comes to you," he teased, kissing the tip of her nose. "How did you get him to relax with a dragon?"

She studied Giaf. He was sitting on the steps, nodding his head to something Pow-pow was telling him. For her, it seemed perfectly natural for the two to be having a conversation. Yet, even back home, such a scene would be unusual. The thought of her home brought a fresh wave of grief.

"I thought you were in meetings until late tonight," she said.

"I stayed for the ones I had to and delegated the others to Adham and Giaf… if he can pull himself away from Pow-pow."

Silence settled between them as they watched Giaf and Pow-pow. Wynter sighed when Khalid slid his arms around her waist and pulled her against him. Her eyes glistened with unshed tears.

"Why does life have to be so complicated?" she wondered aloud.

Khalid kissed her temple, and she released a shuddering breath. The warmth of his lips was soothing. He hugged her tighter.

"What's wrong?" he demanded, turning her to face him.

Biting her lip, she tilted her face away from him. He lifted her chin, forcing her to look at him. She blinked back the tears clouding her vision.

"I've been gone too long. If I don't return soon, my parents are bound to know that something has happened. They will search for me."

Denial flared in his eyes. "You belong here, Wynter, with me."

She closed her eyes and nodded. She needed to go back, to tell her parents what had happened, but what if they tried to stop her from returning to Khalid?

"I have a few more days," she said, opening her eyes and hoping they didn't reveal her lie.

Khalid cupped her cheeks. "We'll have a lifetime together," he vowed.

---

They spent the afternoon together. Khalid remained by her side, as if afraid to let her out of his sight. They ate dinner out in the garden with Ayesha and Giaf. Pow-pow was taking advantage of the new moon to help clean up some of the rubble in the city. Giaf had commented that the residents—and the engineers—had been amazed at how quickly the debris was cleared.

*There's nothing like having a rock-eating dragon when you need to clean up rock,* she mused.

As the sun set, they settled in Faiza's library. Wynter understood why the Queen had loved this room. There was something magical in the décor, like her father Arastan's tomes at home.

On one wall, a row of windows and doors overlooked the garden. Her mother Lyia's garden was much more exotic, the plants from many different worlds, yet, there was the same peacefulness of nature.

"If… you returned to your world, how long would you be gone?" Khalid asked, his voice husky with emotion.

He came up behind her and wrapped his arms around her waist. They were always touching when they were together. Her parents were the same. It was like there was a magnetic force pulling them together. She leaned her head back against his shoulder while she gazed out at the garden.

"Hopefully only a few days. I have a lot of explaining to do to my parents. They…. They aren't aware that I have the powers that I do. When I was little, it was fun having them and my sisters and brothers doing everything. It was like a game. As I grew older, I realized that I was different… not in a bad way, but that I could do more than they could. My game became more of a secret," she said, feeling the weight of her deceit.

"What if I came with you? Is that possible?" he asked.

Her eyes widened. She had never thought about taking Khalid back with her, but that made sense. After all, if she was going to be with him, she would still want to see her family.

"I… don't see why not. Would it be safe for you to leave so soon after everything that has happened?"

Khalid shrugged. "I don't see why not. Adham would oversee things while I'm gone, and my uncle is no longer a threat. I love you, Wynter. All of this… will mean more to me with you by my side. I want to know more about you and your world," he said.

Hope and love soared through her at his declaration. She turned in his arms, rose up, and captured his lips with hers. She wound her arms around his neck as his lips parted and he took control of the kiss. Familiar heat exploded deep in her belly, drawing a moan from her. Their breathing grew louder, more desperate, fed by their fear of being separated.

"We'll make this work," she promised.

With a determined expression in his eyes, Khalid captured her lips in another breath-stealing kiss. Wynter's body melded to his. Sliding her hands down his back, she let the powerful wave of need take over.

*This is where the true magic is.*

The thought no sooner flashed through her mind than she sensed a shift in power—the familiar power of a mage.

She broke away from Khalid and glanced wildly around as the distinctive essence of a magical wave swept over the palace, freezing those caught within the spell. In order to protect Khalid, she needed to know who was creating the spell. She focused. There was no malice in the spell. In fact, she sensed her mother's essence in it.

"Wynter—" Khalid said, his eyes widening as he felt the paralyzing effects of the spell sweeping over him.

Her heart pounded as grief threatened to overwhelm her. Pulling a knife from her boot, she cut a strand of her hair that had come loose and braided it into a bracelet. She tied it around Khalid's wrist, pressing a kiss to the knot to seal it.

"I will return to you… I promise," she said, trying not to cry.

He reached out for her as she stepped away. His hand froze in midair. She turned, following the pull of the magic. It led her back into the garden.

*Your father, mother, and a Mage Council Member,* Pow-pow warned.

The stone dragon landed in front of her, turning with a growl in the direction of an open portal. This one was different from the portals the

Rings of Power created. This portal belonged to Enyo's ancient mages, and it was an incredibly rare sight that very few could manage.

"Wynter," Lyia cried with relief.

Wynter stepped around Pow-pow and looked at her parents and the Mage Council Leader, Eirene. The gray-haired woman dressed in red velvet robes stared back, her eyes widening when she took in Wynter's unusual appearance.

Wynter lifted her chin, regal in her defiance, her power swirling around her. Her body glowed. Her hair lifted and flowed around her as if caught in an underwater current. Power danced between Wynter, Arastan, Lyia, and Eirene, the intensity of which would have terrified this world's humans and most mages.

"So, it is true. The young Princess of Erindale lives," Eirene said, her voice ringing with striking clarity and strength.

# Chapter Twelve

Khalid stumbled forward as the paralysis holding him disappeared. His eyes were wild with confusion and fear when he realized he was alone in the library. He twisted around, frantically searching for Wynter.

He froze when he saw the open French doors. Striding over to them, he stepped out onto the patio and scrutinized the garden. He noted the dazed expressions on Farid and Hagar's faces. They looked as if they were waking from a deep sleep. A moment later, Adham burst through the doorway behind him with an alarmed expression.

Adham frowned, his hand on his sidearm, and turned in a tight circle, searching the garden before facing him again. The older man's eyes held a mixture of fear, caution, and confusion.

"Khalid?"

Khalid shook his head. He had no answers—except that Wynter had disappeared. A muscle pulsed in his jaw. Tension stiffened the muscles in his neck and shoulders. His eyes moved to the gouges in the wall. He paled, feeling a brief flash of rage and then... he just felt hollow.

"She's gone," he said, his voice not quite steady.

"Gone? Where?" Adham replied.

His eyes locked with the other man's, and he clenched his fists as helplessness and hopelessness weighed on his soul. Not since his parents' deaths had he felt this overwhelming sense of despair—as if a void had opened up and swallowed his heart.

"I… don't know," he choked out.

He looked up at the stars. His eyes burned, and his vision blurred. Drawing in a shaky breath, he thought of their kiss, of Wynter's body entangled with his, and he knew that he would never want to taste another woman.

"Come back to me, Wynter," he whispered to the glittering stars. "Come back to me, *janiat alsahra' aljamila*."

---

### Council Chambers for the Order of Enyo

Wynter closed her eyes as she sat between her parents. Her hands were folded in her lap, and while she tried to keep a serene expression on her face, it was hard. A crushing grief was threatening to drag her into a black void. Too much had happened in the past twenty-four hours, and her mind and body felt fragile.

She tearfully looked up at her father when he cupped her hand and squeezed it. His eyes were shadowed with worry and curiosity. She felt so much remorse for hiding her abilities from them.

They all stiffened when the door to the Council room opened. Harmonia stepped out and sent a reassuring smile to their parents. She looked at Wynter, and her smile wavered with uncertainty.

"The Council will see you now," Harmonia said.

"Harmonia," her mother began.

Harmonia touched Lyia's arm. "It will be alright."

Wynter wished she felt confident of that. She pressed a hand to her churning stomach. She really wanted to go home, to Zelos, and crawl into her bed.

*No, what I really want to do is go back to Khalid,* she thought.

She touched the shorter strand of hair near her temple. A vision of him gazing up at the stars formed in her mind, and she swore she could hear his husky voice telling her to come back to him. Tears blurred her vision, and she would have stumbled if not for her father's supportive arm.

"Princess Wynter of Erindale, welcome to the Order of Enyo," Eirene greeted with a bow of her head.

Wynter's eyes moved from council member to council member as they rose from a curved table and bowed their heads to her—all save for one who studied her with a calculating gaze.

At the far end of the platform behind the table was a woman wearing a cyan robe. Her hair was in long dreadlocks and she appeared to be in her mid-fifties, though age was irrelevant among mages. The woman could be two-hundred years old. Power swirled around her. Her expression was neutral, and her stare was unrelenting.

"How do you know... you know about Erindale? How do you know about me?" Wynter demanded in an unsteady voice.

"We've known about you since the day Arastan and Lyia took you in," Eirene said. "The danger was too great to not know. What we aren't sure of is what powers you have—and whether those powers may be a threat to Enyo."

"A threat?" Wynter breathed, staring back at the council members before a sense of deep hurt filled her as she looked at her parents. "Why didn't you tell me?"

"Silence, child!" The order came from the mage at the table who had refused to bow to her.

"You have broken the rules of the Order of Enyo. Do you deny it?" the woman on the platform asked.

"Ceto," Eirene began.

Ceto lifted her hand in dismissal. "She is too dangerous to set free. Until she submits to a full assessment of her powers, I recommend that she be detained."

"Detained? What do you mean detained?" Lyia sputtered with outrage.

"Arastan's research on that world is clear: their mages could rival our own. She is a threat to Enyo," Faunus agreed.

"She also has a rock dragon willing to fight for her," Kyon added.

"Wynter is no threat to anyone," Arastan argued.

"The rock dragon has never harmed a soul and lives peacefully on Zelos," Lyia protested. "I've studied Pow-pow extensively over the past fourteen years, and he is a peaceful beast."

"You've also observed this child for the past eighteen years and were unaware of her powers," Ceto replied.

"Council members, Wynter and her pet have never shown any aggression," Eirene interjected in a calming voice.

"How many times has she threatened the Mage-line by using these illegal Rings of Power as a portal? How many worlds has she corrupted or destroyed through her carelessness?" Ceto demanded.

Wynter was shaking her head. "Please, I didn't mean any harm."

"I vote that Wynter Stormhold be arrested and the stone dragon destroyed. Who agrees?" Ceto asked.

"NO!" Wynter cried with horror.

"Ceto! There is no need—" Eirene gasped.

"Please, Your Graces. Wynter is harmless," Arastan protested in alarm.

"You can't do this! Pow-pow never harmed anyone. How can you kill him? At least send him back to his world," Wynter objected, fighting against the guards who came closer to detain her.

"The creature knows too much of mages and the worlds that you have traveled to. You are the one who has condemned him," Ceto declared.

Eirene turned to her peers. "This has not been voted on, Ceto. I strongly object and vote nay on both orders."

Ceto turned to the other three members of the council, her eyes flashing. Two members voted in agreement with Ceto. Only one, Phaunos, shook his head and said nay.

"Three-to-two in favor. Take her away," Ceto ordered.

Wynter was horrified, and her family was stunned. Harmonia was shaking her head and holding onto their parents' arms, begging them to be calm. Fear for them burst through Wynter along with the need to protect Pow-pow.

"Move it along," the guard said, cuffing her wrists in magic-restraining cuffs and pushing against her lower back.

Wynter stumbled as they exited the council room. Fear almost paralyzed her. Behind her, she could hear her parents pleading and Eirene demanding to know what right Ceto had to make such outlandish claims. She peered under her eyelashes. She was surrounded by guards.

*Pow-pow, hide,* she warned.

*Break free. We fly away,* Pow-pow growled.

*I can't until I know my family is safe. Don't let them catch you. I... will come as soon as I can,* she replied.

*They no catch me.*

She sniffed and lifted her shoulder to wipe away the tear rolling down her cheek. The guard ahead of her opened a door that led to a set of dark, spiraling stone steps. Her heart beating wildly, Wynter stepped through the doorway and began her terrifying descent.

---

The faint clicks of heels on stone woke Wynter three days later. She sat up and tiredly rubbed her eyes. Rising from the rickety cot, she walked over to the door and gripped the bars. Her eyes widened when she saw her sister's worried face.

"Harmonia, what are you doing here?" she hissed.

"I wanted to tell you that Father and Mother have returned to Zelos. Ceto has banished them and ordered that all of Father's Rings of Power be confiscated."

"What is going on? *Why* is Ceto— Why would she….?"

Harmonia glanced over her shoulder before leaning closer. "Ceto has always resented Eirene's influence. She's tired of fighting diplomatically with other mages. She wants the Rings of Power, and she needs you to show her how to turn them into a portal. No one else can do that. With you and the rings, she can take control of an infinite number of more primitive worlds where no one will challenge her."

"How did she know I was from Erindale?" Wynter muttered.

"I don't know. All I know is that Ceto has ordered the guards to bring you to the tower at midnight," Harmonia whispered.

"What's in the tower?" Wynter whispered back.

"The Mind Mirror," Eirene answered. "Whatever happens, it must not be used on Wynter."

Harmonia bit back a cry of dismay when Eirene stepped out of the shadows behind her. Wynter wanted to reach out and grip her sister's hand. Instead, she warily waited for whatever Eirene would do.

Eirene surprised both of them when she waved her hand over the locking mechanism. The door Wynter had been holding disappeared, and she stumbled forward. Harmonia held her steady.

"We must leave quickly before the guards realize that you have escaped," Eirene said.

"I… what about you and Harmonia? Will you get in trouble for helping me?" Wynter asked.

Eirene's lips curled into an almost cruel smile. "Ceto would never dare accuse me of such a devious thing, and Harmonia is currently being seen upstairs enjoying dinner."

"Oh," Wynter muttered.

"Come along. We don't have much time," Eirene ordered.

Wynter followed Eirene, and Harmonia took up the rear. Eirene led them to the end of the corridor, then reached up and ran her hands along the rough stone. An opening appeared revealing a spiral stairwell.

The steps seemed to go on forever. When they reached the upper parapet, Eirene held up her hand, then motioned for them to follow her.

"You will need to hide far away until I've dealt with Ceto. You cannot go back to Zelos. I need you to take these and protect them," Eirene said, holding out a medium-size sack.

"What is it?" Wynter asked, taking the bag.

"Your father's Rings of Power," Eirene replied with a smirk.

"Where should I go?" she asked, looking into the bag.

"Move around, often. Pow-pow will join you."

Wynter looked up at Eirene. "How will I know when it is safe to come home?"

Eirene's eyes softened with compassion. "Give me your hand."

Wynter offered her hand. Eirene held it between her two hands, closed her eyes and whispered an incantation. Wynter gasped when she felt a pain burn through her palm in a concentrated spear. Eirene's grasp tightened when Wynter tried to pull away. Only when the pain subsided did Eirene release her. Wynter blinked away her tears and studied her palm.

"A mark will appear when it is safe. It may take time, Wynter. Ceto's deceit has woven deeper than I first realized. Go quickly. Be careful, and at the first hint of danger, travel to another world. Harmonia, signal Pow-pow."

Wynter nodded and Harmonia casted an elegant signal with her hands. Seconds later, Wynter heard the familiar swish of Pow-pow's wings. Eirene gave her a fierce hug.

"Be safe, child. I know not how long it may be until we meet again," Eirene whispered.

Harmonia sniffed and hugged her quickly. "I'll watch over mom and dad," she promised.

Wynter nodded. "I love you, Harmonia," she said.

Pow-pow landed on the parapet. Wynter hurried over and climbed onto his back. Alarms sounded.

"Go, Pow-pow," Wynter instructed.

She clutched the bag of rings in one hand and Pow-pow's spinal plate in the other. Pow-pow lifted off with a mighty burst. The upper tower guards began a fiery attack. Reaching into the bag, she grabbed a ring and hoped the other side was a habitable place. She tossed the ring in front of them and willed it open. Her breath caught when she saw a lush world with giant mushrooms.

Pow-pow dove for the portal as a group of guards in flying machines advanced. Wynter reached out behind her, palm extended, and commanded the ring into her hand, closing the portal a split second before a volley of powerful blasts struck.

# Chapter Thirteen

**Six months later:**

Wynter cursed under her breath, gripped Pow-pow tightly with her legs, and held onto his spinal plate as they plunged through a thick forest in yet another world. Behind them, Ceto's mercenary guards pursued her. Pow-pow released a powerful burst of stone spikes from his mouth. The spikes shattered the trunk of a massive tree. The stone dragon passed under the tree as it fell. A loud explosion behind them told Wynter that one of the mercenaries had been stopped.

*Two more to go,* Pow-pow said, swerving when a blast swept too close for comfort.

They broke through the edge of the forest over a steep cliff. This world was filled with reptiles twice the size of Pow-pow. Some were herbivores, but some were absolutely omnivores or carnivores. Being out in the open was dangerous.

*Pow-pow, on your left!* Wynter warned.

A large flying carnivore had spotted them. She pressed herself closer to Pow-pow's neck.

A blast struck the dragon's side, sending him into a steep spiral. The scent of scorched rock wafted around them.

The two mercenaries were gaining on them. Wynter glanced back and forth. On one side was the bird of prey, its colorful twenty-foot wingspan, three-foot talons, and serrated beak swerving toward them. On the other, a mercenary with a magical shield and a plasma rifle.

Wynter locked her knees against Pow-pow's hard plates and held out her arms, sending a stream of electrical current in both directions. The bird of prey veered away from the electrifying stream. The mercenary didn't move quite fast enough. A bolt hit the fuselage of his flying machine and it exploded. Out of the corner of her eye, she saw the man fall.

"If the explosion or fall doesn't kill him, the creatures on this world will," she muttered with no sympathy.

She had lost all feelings of sympathy five-and-a-half months ago. Now she wanted all of them to crash and burn. Glancing over her shoulder, she saw the other mercenary gaining on Pow-pow. Bursts of laser fire peppered the air around them as Pow-pow dodged then pulled up and swung his tail. The hard rock club on the end of his tail connected with the flying machine, shattering it.

The rider activated his flying pack. Pieces of the flaming machine rained down to the forest below, and a shadow passed overhead. The bird of prey soared in their direction, and Pow-pow veered to the left. She shuddered when the gigantic bird caught the mercenary between its beak and broke the man in half.

"Oh, gross," she exclaimed, turning her head.

"Better him than us," Pow-pow replied.

"True. We'd better take cover. It will be dark soon and there will only be more birds out."

Pow-pow grunted in agreement. Wynter held on tightly as Pow-pow dived. There were dangers in the forest below, but at least they had places they could hide. Pow-pow weaved through the forest before landing on a thick branch thirty feet above the ground.

"We need to move to a new world," Wynter sighed.

Pow-pow helped her slide off his back and stand on the branch. He kept his wing partially folded around her as she picked her way to the trunk of the tree. She was exhausted.

"I don't like this world," he muttered.

She slid down until she was sitting and stretched her legs out. Pow-pow rested his head next to her, and she gently caressed his jaw. Leaning her head back, she stared up at the stars through a break in the canopy. Night-time fell fast on this world.

"I wonder if he is happy," she murmured.

Pow-pow lifted his head. "We could go there next."

Tears burned her eyes. "You know we can't do that. Ceto has found us in every world we've traveled to. I don't dare lead her to Khalid."

Pow-pow grunted in disagreement. "You miss him."

"Yes, I do."

The next morning, she pulled a ring out that she had only visited once before—the ring to Erindale. There was no one there that Ceto could hurt—at least not in the castle. If she could not go to Khalid, then at least she could go home. Dare she risk returning to Erindale?

It was time to make a stand. She was done with running and hiding.

"Are you ready? I smell a predator nearby." Pow-pow mumbled, warily turning his head.

"Yes, let's go."

Wynter stood outside of Tomas and LaNie's barn two weeks later. She hadn't planned on coming to the couple she had met months ago. If it hadn't been for Desiree, she wouldn't have. The young girl had discovered her and Pow-pow near the river.

"Good morning, Your Highness," Desiree greeted with a curtsy.

Wynter laughed and shook her head. "Will you ever call me just Wynter?"

"No. How is Master Pow-pow this fine morning?"

Pow-pow smacked his lips, yawned, and stretched. His tail knocked into a small rock wall near the barn, causing it to tumble. He grimaced and started placing the fallen rocks back into a pile.

"I'm doing well, Mistress Desiree," Pow-pow cheerfully responded. "It is nice to wake in a place where everything isn't trying to eat us."

Desiree nodded. "I was going down to the river to check the fish traps. Would you like to see if you can find some clay this morning?"

Pow-pow's bright green eyes twinkled with delight, and he looked at Wynter.

"Go have fun. We can travel to the castle when you return," she said.

Pow-pow turned a mischievous grin to Desiree. "Would you like a ride to the river?"

Desiree's lips parted in awe, and she vigorously nodded. "Oh, that would be wonderful!"

Wynter laughed. "He's only offering because he's hungry."

Desiree reached out and stroked Pow-pow's neck. "I know where there is a big clay deposit," she loudly whispered.

Wynter stood back as the dragon and the very excited young mage on his back bounded off. She waited until they were out of sight before she walked over to the cottage. The door opened a split second before she arrived.

"Good morning, Your Highness," Tomas greeted.

"Good morning, Tomas. I was wondering if I could talk with you and LaNie."

"It would be an honor," Tomas answered.

---

Tomas and LaNie told Wynter that her mother, Queen Larenta, was considered the most powerful mage on the planet. They explained that Erindale was their capital, and smaller kingdoms were scattered throughout the lands.

Each kingdom was led by a small group of mages. LaNie and Tomas had been part of the council for one of these kingdoms. Wynter's mother had come from a line of mages known as the Illumini who were said to have come to this world thousands of years ago.

"The first Illumini helped bring peace to our planet. They shared their skills, and their blood. Over time, the people of this world and the Illumini became one. Prophecies tell of a child born with hair the color of lightning threaded with pure energy. She will be the most powerful of all and rule as protector," LaNie explained.

Tomas nodded. "You have the power to bring back those turned to stone and restore the capital of Nysus."

Wynter stared at the couple. "How?"

"You will know what to do when the time is right." LaNie placed her hand over Wynter's heart. "It's within you. It's your birthright."

"Take care, though," Tomas warned. "Everyone who enters Erindale turns to stone."

When Wynter told them that she and Pow-pow had already entered the city and they were just fine, LaNie replied that it must be because she was the rightful heir to the throne.

"Spells can be funny that way," LaNie said. "We tend to think that friendship and alliances are separate from magic, but magic has a way of grouping together people who share love and understanding. Your ancient blood clearly protected you from the stone curse—and your companion was included in that protection, or perhaps Pow-pow refraining from turning to stone is not that complicated." She laughed. "He is already made of stone, is he not?"

A short while later, Wynter and Pow-pow left for the castle, and during the flight, she fidgeted with the end of her braid as she mulled over her conversation with LaNie and Tomas.

*You will know what to do when the time is right.*

LaNie's words reminded her so much of Khalid. He had known when it was the right time to take back his rightful place, and he had fought for it. She touched the ring around her neck and felt mental anguish so intense, it took her breath away.

*We should go to him,* Pow-pow insisted, feeling her strong emotions.

*When it is safe. I will not endanger him.*

Pow-pow snorted and shook his head. Wynter breathed a sigh of relief when the castle came into view. Pow-pow raced along the outer rampart. The air sizzled with the magic protecting the kingdom.

The statues of the men standing on the wall's platforms caught her attention—especially the one standing at the center. She recognized him as her biological father, both from the vision she had years ago and the way she felt drawn to him.

"Take me to the balcony," she requested.

Pow-pow turned and glided higher. They crossed over the wall. Wynter felt a change in the air when they passed through the magic. A surge of power went through her, and she stiffened as her skin radiated light and her hair swirled as if it had a life of its own. She felt… energized.

"What is it?" Pow-pow asked.

Knowledge flowed through her mind, an ancient knowledge that had been passed down to each generation of Illumini. She saw visions and heard words spoken in a language older than the Mage-line of Enyo.

*"Awake, my people, for I have returned. Peace be with us once again."*

The words flowed from her mouth as Pow-pow circled over the palace. As she spoke, her power mingled with the energy held in place by the twelve silent sentinels.

The magic rolled backwards, sweeping over the frozen residents of Erindale. Rock turned to ash, leaving dazed and confused residents stumbling.

By the time Pow-pow landed on the balcony that had once belonged to her parents' living quarters, the kingdom had awakened. The residents of the kingdom turned as one and looked up at the princess with snow-white hair sitting atop a stone dragon. She glowed with power and her gaze promised protection and love.

A burning in her palm drew her attention to her hand. She stared at the magical mark with eyes filled with tears. Ceto's reign of terror had ended. Wynter could go home. Looking out over the kingdom, her gaze paused on her father, and she knew that this was where she belonged.

---

**Earth: Deion**

Khalid reined in his powerful stallion and instinctively touched the braided bracelet on his wrist. It was glowing again. Each time it did, he hoped it was a signal of Wynter's return.

*And each time, she never does.*

No matter how often he scolded himself for wishing, he continued to believe that she would come back. He closed his eyes. It had been six months. The emptiness made it feel like years.

"You felt her again," Giaf asked, reining in his horse beside Khalid's.

He nodded, removing his hand. Wynter's hair glowed in the darkness. He could feel her emotions—fear, fatigue, hope, sadness, and most suffocating of all, loneliness. For a while, he wondered if the emotions were a magnification of his own.

"What do you sense this time?" Giaf asked.

"Peace." He tilted his head to stare up at the stars.

Giaf frowned. "Do you think she is alright?"

"Yes." He looked at the bracelet again. "If something had happened to her, the light would have faded."

Over the past six months, he had dreamed almost nightly of Wynter. He had often woken drenched in sweat and trembling with fear, his heart pounding so hard that he was surprised it didn't burst through his chest.

The dreams had been filled with terrifying creatures and the constant threat of danger. He recognized that she was trying to shield him as best she could, but he was connected to Wynter. He knew in his soul that she would have returned to him if she could, but she would never do so if it would endanger him or this world.

And so he waited.

"We'd best be getting back before Dhat-Badan sends a search party out for us," Giaf said, pulling him back to the present.

"Yes."

They rode back to Deion in silence. The past six months, Khalid had turned his focus on rebuilding his country. Most of the external scars left from his uncle's rule had been repaired, but there were still the internal ones that would take longer. There were still people who distrusted him because of his blood connection to Inarus.

A meeting between the tribal leaders throughout his country had been organized by Dhat-Badan in the ancient city of Deion. She was well respected by everyone, and he had agreed with her counsel that he needed to meet—and listen—to the concerns in a neutral place of trust.

They had gathered here three days ago. After endless rounds of meetings, he needed to escape into the quietness of the desert. It was here that he could let down his guard and remember the nights he had spent with Wynter, making love to her under the brilliant blanket of stars.

*Come back to me, janiat alsahra' aljamila,* he silently pleaded, stroking the ribbon of hair tied around his wrist. He hoped she heard him.

# Chapter Fourteen

**Present Day: Erindale**

Wynter stood on her balcony watching the chaos of merchants and pedestrians going about their daily lives. A cool breeze lifted the wisps of hair around her face. She brushed her hair back and closed her eyes. A faint plea swept through her mind.

*Oh, Khalid,* she thought.

A noise behind her broke the connection. She startled and opened her eyes.

"Your morning tea, Your Highness. Would you like anything else?" Desiree asked.

Wynter returned the young teen's infectious smile. Fourteen-year-old Desiree was going to be a heartbreaker, and her talents were growing under the tutelage of Wynter's sister, Electra.

"No, thank you, Desiree. How are your studies coming along?" she inquired, crossing the room to pour herself a cup of tea.

"Wonderful. We are working on Botanical Magic. It is my favorite," Desiree replied.

"That will be all, Desiree," Eirene stated placidly. "Electra was asking for you in the nursery."

"Yes, ma'am," Desiree said with a curtsy. She rolled her eyes before she exited the room.

Wynter's lips twitched with mirth. She lifted her cup to her lips to conceal her expression, though she seriously doubted that Eirene had missed the teen's reaction.

Eirene rolled her own eyes and poured herself a cup of tea. Wynter laughed, and together, they walked onto the balcony. Neither spoke as they watched the miracle below them. So much had changed overnight for Erindale.

Pow-pow had been extremely helpful in cleaning away the destruction —calling it snack time as he gobbled away at the fallen stone. Wynter's smile faded as she thought about the last few months and how much her life had changed.

"How are your parents?" Eirene inquired.

"Good. Father has found several new worlds to observe. Mother has been working with Electra in the new botanical magic classes. Both Father and mother enjoy living here. I was surprised when Electra decided to join us as well. She and Mother are really enjoying teaching. They all say the power contained here is much stronger than any other world they have visited."

Eirene nodded. "How is your relationship with your biological father?"

Wynter hesitated before she answered. "It has been... difficult, but things are getting better. I can feel his sadness. He misses my mother."

"I can imagine. You bring great joy to his life, though. He loves you," Eirene said.

Wynter nodded. "I know. I have so many memories that aren't mine. It is overwhelming. I still can't believe he and the others are alive. If only...."

Her voice faded as she thought of her birth mother, Queen Larenta. Wynter looked so much like her that it was difficult for Everes to look at her.

She gazed out over the kingdom. It would take years of intense study to come into her full magical abilities and learn how to control them. The memories of the ancients crowded her mind. Until she learned to categorize them, much like her father did with the tomes he created, it would be difficult for her to focus on what to learn first.

Ultimately, breaking the spell cast by her mother had turned out to be the easy part. LaNie had been right, the knowledge had come to her. The return of the king without his queen had been heartbreaking. The meeting of his daughter was both joyous and crushingly sad.

Wynter wasn't sure she would have survived if it hadn't been for her adoptive parents and Eirene. Ceto had almost destroyed the Order of Enyo with an attempted assassination of the other members of the council. Eirene was the one who stopped her, entombing Ceto in the dark realm, an isolated prison for mages, where she could do no more harm.

Only then had Eirene activated the spell on Wynter's hand to let her know that it was safe to return.

"If only...?" Eirene gently inquired.

Wynter lifted a delicate shoulder and shook her head. She missed Khalid. Their connection was something she treasured, and her heart would always belong to him, but she knew her place was here. Her duty was to her people. She understood how he felt now.

Eirene studied her with a sympathetic expression and waved her hand towards the kingdom below. "Your mother's sacrifice allowed them to live, but it is more than the loss of your mother that causes you pain."

Wynter winced. The mage saw too much. Wynter turned away from Eirene.

"Wynter—" Everes said as he stepped onto the balcony. "My apologies for the interruption, Mage Eirene," he greeted.

"Your Majesty. It is always a pleasure to see you. Wynter, I need to return to Enyo. If you need anything, send for me," Eirene said with a compassionate smile.

"I know. Thank you for everything, Eirene."

Everes was silent until Eirene left. Wynter studied her biological father's face. Grief had etched deep lines around his mouth and shadowed his eyes. As he studied her, the lines eased and love replaced the shadows.

"You've done wonders," she said with a nod of her head toward the city.

"None of this could have happened without you," he replied.

Wynter had been debating for a while about how much she should tell him about her vision. They had avoided this conversation. Actually, they had avoided any personal discussion at all. Their emotions had been too raw. They had needed time to come to terms with everything that had happened and what the future might hold.

She thought it might be time now, and the hesitant yet determined expression on Everes's face could mean that he felt the same way. The question was which of them would take the first step.

She gripped the stone railing and bit her lip.

*Maybe knowing might ease some of his grief,* she thought.

*You should tell him.*

Pow-pow's encouraging words made her smile. She looked up and saw him on one of the turrets, sealing some stones with molten dragon spit. He peered over his shoulder at her and winked. She smiled, and took a deep breath.

"I saw her.... I saw mother... when I came here the first time," she confessed.

Her father stiffened. "How?"

"I'm not sure. It was a vision, but I connected with her in some tangible way, as if a part of her was really here... or a part of me—the adult version of me, not just the baby me—was really there.... Anyway... I saw you and her together... before—" She shook her head, her hair loosening from the bun she had it in. "She gave the last of her power to save you, this world... and me. When my father.... Arastan was watching what happened. Mother could sense that the Rings of Power could make a portal, not just a window. Dad had never tried to go through one before. She got him to promise that he would protect me, and she sent me through."

"I'm glad," he said, meeting her eyes. "If not, I would have lost you as well."

They smiled. Silence stretched for a few moments.

"I loved your mother very much," he sighed, the weariness of grief evident in his whole demeanor. "Having you here at least gives me a wonderful part of her."

He covered her hand with his own. Tears burned Wynter's eyes, and she bit her lip again to keep from crying. Her vision blurred.

"I love someone," she confessed.

She looked up at him, her eyes filled with confusion. He brushed the loose strands of her hair away from her face.

"But you aren't happy. There is a problem?" he asked.

"I need to be here and he's not here and we've been apart for so long and it hurts so much," she said in a rush.

"Oh, Wynter. I am the King of Erindale. Since you brought me back, you are the princess. What is a princess if she is not happy? What kind of king would I be if I could not grant my daughter the same happiness I once shared with your mother?" he questioned with a gentle smile.

Hope and uncertainty filled her. Was it that simple? But... Khalid's world—could she ever fit in there? Would he accept hers?

"Go to him. Life is too fleeting to not fight for something so precious," he encouraged.

She gave Everes a watery smile and threw her arms around his neck. He swept her close, burying his face against her hair and hugging her back. A shudder ran through both of them. This was the first time they had hugged each other. A low sob slipped from her, and she buried her face against his chest.

"I love you, daughter. I look forward to meeting the man who has captured your heart. Erindale... and I will be here for you when you return," Everes vowed, rubbing her back.

"Thank you," she whispered, her voice tight with emotion. "I... *love you, daddy.*" she said in the old language.

*"I love you, my daughter."*

Wynter pulled away from her father. Pow-pow, with his keen hearing and awareness of her emotions, launched himself from the turret and soared over to the balcony. Wynter sat on the edge of the railing and swung her legs over. The moment Pow-pow was underneath, she pushed off.

She landed on his back, gripping the dragon's scales. They were becoming smoother every day. Her father leaned over the railing, his eyes shining with love. A trembling smile curved her lips when he bowed his head.

"Go, Wynter. I want to hold my grandchild soon," he chuckled.

Wynter flushed and grinned. She pulled the ring from around her neck, and Pow-pow wiggled with excitement.

"Hang on," Pow-pow instructed.

"Fly like the wind, Pow-pow," she laughed, bending over his neck.

With a burst of speed that drew gasps from the people below, the stone dragon shot forward, a rumble of thunder following in his wake. Workmen cursed the dragon when tiles crumbled and fell in the shockwave.

Once they were past the walls of the castle, Wynter tossed the ring and opened the portal. Hope and excitement filled her. They would be together, and nothing, absolutely nothing would stop them.

# Chapter Fifteen

**Earth: Present Day**

"How do we know he can be trusted!" an angry voice shouted above the crowd.

"He is rebuilding the country," Giaf retorted.

"My people starve while he lives in a palace. I don't see how the rebuilding has helped us," another sheikh snapped.

"I heard he has taken the daughters of prominent businessmen and plans to keep them for himself!" someone yelled.

Khalid and Adham shared a commiserating look. More than a hundred people were gathered around nomadic tribe leaders. Mixed among them were his cabinet members, the prominent businessmen whose daughters he had supposedly absconded with, and trusted foreign associates who were willing to invest in Aethon.

"I think some of the old ways should be reconsidered. Can we just go back to killing idiots who make stupid comments?" Adham muttered.

Khalid pursed his lips to keep from laughing. If anyone heard him agreeing with Adham's joke, they might take it seriously and add it to the long list of other sins he had supposedly committed. Instead of responding, he breathed deeply and counted.

Sheikh Qavus-Malka, leader of the Taniyn Mountain tribe stepped forward. The man was in his early fifties, he was taller than Khalid by several inches and outweighed him by a good forty pounds—and it was all muscle. He carried a staff topped with a long, curved claw, said to have come from a dragon that once protected Aethon.

In reality, it was the claw of a velociraptor or some other type of dinosaur that once roamed the Earth. Now that Khalid had seen a real dragon, he knew there was no comparison. He took a deep breath and held onto the memory of Wynter, lifting his eyes to the stars above until the hollow feeling in his chest disappeared.

"There can only be one true ruler of Aethon," Qavus-Malka declared.

Everyone went silent.

"And who makes that decision, Qavus? You?" Sheikh R'ad Saifullah demanded.

Qavus glared across the fire at the other sheikh. "Why not? I hold the power of the dragon. According to ancient law, the one who holds the dragon can challenge for the throne."

"That is not true, Qavus," Dhat-Badan said, rising from her seat. "The ancient law states that the king must find a bride by his twenty-ninth year. If he does not, then the one who holds the dragon's claw may select his bride for him."

Qavus's eyes narrowed. "His twenty-nineth birthday approaches, and he has no bride."

"What does it matter that his birthday is approaching? That isn't even a dragon's claw!" Giaf snapped. "It is from a dinosaur."

Qavus's eyes flashed, and he slammed the end of his staff into the ground. "You wouldn't know a dragon's claw from a hole in the ground even if it bit you in the butt. This is a dragon's claw," he growled.

Giaf scoffed and folded his arms across his chest. "No, it is not. That is a child's toenail compared to a real dragon's claw."

"How would you know? It isn't like you've ever seen a real dragon," the man next to Qavus mockingly retorted.

"Oh, I've seen a real dragon. That little thing is not a dragon's claw!"

"What type of king surrounds himself with liars? One who would cheat and steal from his people like his uncle did!" Qavus sneered.

"Actually, Giaf is correct. That is not a dragon's claw," a smooth, husky voice remarked.

Khalid stiffened. His heart hammered against his chest. Almost afraid to believe his ears, he slowly swiveled on his heel.

The crowd parted as if pushed by invisible hands. Through the gap, an ethereal figure with shimmering white hair walked toward him. Her eyes were locked on his face, her lips curved in a trembling smile.

He swallowed past the lump in his throat. She was just as beautiful as he remembered. Afraid to truly believe that she was there, he tentatively stretched out his hand, and she matched him, her fingers sliding along his palm. He grabbed her hand hard and pulled her closer until she stood touching him. They stared at each other, oblivious to everyone watching.

"I have missed you so much," she murmured as she caressed his cheek.

His breath rushed out of him, leaving him dizzy. His fingers trembled as he caressed her cheek and slid his hand into her hair. They moved forward at the same time, kissing passionately.

It wasn't until Adham cleared his throat that he reluctantly released her. Even then, he continued to gaze into her shimmering emerald eyes. She touched the braided bracelet wrapped around his wrist.

"You came back to me," he breathed in an unsteady voice.

"Always," she replied.

"Who is this woman?" Qavus demanded.

Khalid didn't look at the man as he replied. "She is my betrothed," he declared.

His announcement created an uproar that rippled through the crowd. The only ones who remained silent were the few who knew the truth about Wynter.

"You would soil the bloodlines of Aethon with a commoner? A foreigner who will weaken the royal house?" Qavus demanded.

"Sheikh Qavus-Malka is right. You must marry a princess," Sheikh R'ad Saifullah said.

The murmur of agreement in the crowd finally pulled Khalid's attention from Wynter. He tightened his grip on her hand as he faced the crowd. Anger surged inside him. He had lost his parents to this country. He had fought to bring it back from the edge of despair. He had bled, sweated, and given everything to his people. The one thing he would not give up was Wynter.

"I am a princess," Wynter said, smiling at the men who wanted to tear her away from the man she loved.

"You are no princess," Qavus scoffed, eyeing her long dark brown coat, white shirt, trousers, and boots with disdain.

"She is a child of the desert. She is 'amirat khurafiat alsahra," Dhat-Badan stated.

Wynter smiled. "Hello, my friend," she greeted.

"It is good that you have returned. You can open these idiots' eyes and prevent them from making the biggest mistake of their lives," Dhat-Badan said.

Of course, the 'idiots' were outraged by Dhat-Badan's comments. Wynter chuckled and turned mischievous eyes to the men who were turning red in the face. She tilted her head, her eyes on the claw at the end of the staff.

"Would you like to see what a real dragon's claw looks like?" she asked.

The crowd quieted, staring at her as if she had lost her mind. Behind her, Khalid chuckled while Giaf and Adham snickered.

"Wynter…," Khalid cautioned.

She lifted her hand and looked at him over her shoulder. "Trust me. If all else fails, my father is excited to meet you."

He waved his hand in a motion for her to continue. Perhaps a little shock value would go a long way in silencing the critics challenging his every decision.

A growl came from beyond the ring of people gathered around the fire. The rumble caused the desert sands under their feet to vibrate and shift. Several in the group looked toward the protective wall of the city, debating if they could escape behind the massive walls. Others glanced nervously out into the darkness of the sands. The few who stood in defiance scowled with unease.

"What kind of trick is this?" Qavus demanded, glancing back and forth between Wynter and Khalid.

"Pow-pow, would you be so kind as to show Sheikh Qavus what a real dragon's claw looks like?"

A rumbling chuckle drew gasps and cries from the crowd. People shoved each other as they scooted away from the sound, their eyes round with fear as they scanned the darkness in the direction of the amused laugh.

"With pleasure, Your Highness," the invisible dragon replied.

The ground shook as Pow-pow stepped forward through the gap in the crowd that had been left when Wynter arrived. Khalid smiled. He knew from experience that the dragon could walk lightly enough to barely leave a trace in the sand. The stomp had to be for effect.

Qavus's eyes narrowed with suspicion as he gazed across the fire at them. Heat radiated off the dragon's body, and Khalid knew if he were to stretch his hand out, he would touch Pow-pow's hard scales.

Giaf and Adham must have felt the unusual warmth as well, because they did reach out, their palms laying flat against Pow-pow before they jerked their hands away and scooted several steps to the side.

"You think to make a fool of me?" Qavus accused Wynter.

"I think you are doing a good enough job on your own," Pow-pow responded. He materialized less than a foot in front of Qavus. In the midst of the cries of horror, screams of terror, and a lot of praying, Pow-pow said, "By the way, this is what a real dragon's claw looks like." He lifted his front right foot and extended his long claws.

Given Qavus's expression, Khalid was surprised the man's eyes didn't fall out. Pow-pow's lips curved into a mischievous smile, displaying a very impressive row of foot-long, razor-sharp teeth. When the rest of the dragon's body solidified, Khalid noticed that Pow-pow had grown —a lot—since he had last seen him.

More than a dozen people fainted, and Khalid noticed a few 'accidents'.

"May I introduce you to my friend, Pow-pow. He is a stone dragon," Wynter said.

Khalid was impressed that his people didn't run into the desert in an all-out panic. He stepped forward, running his hand along Pow-pow's side.

Qavus's eyes rolled back in his head as he fainted, the staff with the dinosaur's claw falling to the ground beside him. Pow-pow leaned down and sniffed Qavus. He shook his head.

"He's going to need some clean underwear when he wakes up," Pow-pow commented with distaste.

Dhat-Badan stepped forward and bowed low to Pow-pow. The dragon returned her bow with a graceful dip of his head, his emerald eyes glittering with mirth.

"The *rakib altiniyn* has returned!" she proclaimed, turning and lifting her hands into the air.

Her proclamation that the Dragon Rider had returned was greeted with silence for several seconds before Ayesha, Wahida, Imad, and Zaki began whooping loudly in a joyful cheer. Giaf and Adham joined in. Soon, those that had not fainted or run to their tents joined in, too.

Pow-pow, caught up in the excitement, lifted his head and released a loud roar before banging his tail enthusiastically on the ground. The vibration and noise startled the horses, camels, and other animals. Khalid heard Wynter whisper a word and lift her hands. In seconds, the animals calmed. Pow-pow shot him a sheepish look and winked.

"I like your people," Pow-pow said with a rumble of laughter.

# Epilogue

Wynter leaned back against Khalid and watched the people surrounding Pow-pow. The stone dragon was eating up all the attention. He was currently answering Qavus's endless round of questions. Children were crawling all over him while teenagers tried to lift his tail in a contest to see who was the strongest.

"I have to admit, my people handled this much better than I expected. Of course, they don't know what *you* can do yet," Khalid mused.

Wynter giggled and nodded. "Me, too. I think we'll wait awhile before we tell them I'm an alien."

She tilted her head back, needing to feel Khalid's lips against hers again. He cradled her in his arms. He was happy to prove that neither of them was dreaming. She sighed with contentment.

Khalid ran his fingers along her cheek, and she captured his hand, holding his strong fingers against her flushed skin.

"What happened?" he finally asked.

The tremor of vulnerability and uncertainty in his voice made her heart hurt. She outlined his lips with the tip of her index finger. Remembered loneliness threatened to choke her.

"So much… too much," she confessed, her eyes moving from his face to the stars above. She told him everything about her capture and her escape, and then came the hard part of the story. She tried to describe it as briefly as possible.

"Ceto discovered that she could find me using my father's tomes. I didn't realize that each Ring of Power is spellbound to the tome that describes it. Pow-pow and I were forced to flee from world to world to world. Ceto's mercenaries always found us. I couldn't bring them here, so I stayed away."

A tear slid down her cheek. Khalid caught it on the tip of his finger and placed it on his tongue.

He jerked back in surprise, his eyes dilating as her memories flashed through his mind in vivid detail. She held his hand to her chest while he panted and then took slow, deep breaths as the scenes faded.

Wynter bit her lip and captured his pale face between her palms. He blinked several times before he took in one last shuddering breath and focused on her face.

"Your world… your mother…." He fought to process everything that had happened to her.

She nodded, stroking his face gently as his pulse slowed. He glanced at Pow-pow who was watching them with a calm expression.

Wynter opened her mouth to ask Khalid if he was alright, but the words never formed because he captured her lips, kissing her with a desperate passion that left her aching with need. Wild thoughts flashed through her mind, and she wondered if they could sneak away.

"I have a tent set up. Do you think Pow-pow can handle this on his own?" Khalid asked, his voice husky with need.

Wynter glanced over her shoulder. Pow-pow was the hit of the night. She seriously doubted anyone would miss them.

"I think he can keep everyone entertained for as long as we need."

Khalid stood up, pulling Wynter to her feet alongside him before he swept her into his arms. She wound her arms around his neck with a giggle of delight.

"Good. We may be busy for a long, long time," he retorted.

Wynter smiled and rested her head against Khalid's shoulder. She would ask him to meet her family tomorrow. They would have many more tomorrows—in both their worlds.

I hope you enjoyed Wynter and the Stone Dragon! This story actually has Easter Eggs to two other series that I have written, my *Magic, New Mexico* series and my *Seven Kingdoms* series. I love writing stories that are interconnected, and I love discovering new and exciting stories to share with you! Read on to learn more.

Touch of Frost
*Book 1 of Magic, New Mexico*

Frost is a Star Ranger. He travels the star systems bringing intergalactic fugitives to justice. When a maximum-security fugitive escapes from the mining prison, it is Frost who is sent after him—only this time, the fugitive has escaped to a distant, forbidden planet. Now Frost is in a race to find the fugitive before the natives of Earth discover them!

Lacey Adams lives in the small town of Magic, New Mexico where she devotes herself to her Touch of Magic Animal Shelter. The animals help heal the pain and loneliness inside her since the death of her husband three years ago. Magic is an *unusual* town, to say the least, but she has never met an alien before, and now there are two in her home!

When Lacey is taken hostage, Frost is shocked to discover that his heart is not as frozen as he thought and Lacey is a far more formidable opponent than either he or the fugitive could have imagined. Find out what happens when Frost makes a decision guaranteed to put him on the Most Wanted list... he follows his heart and kidnaps Lacey.

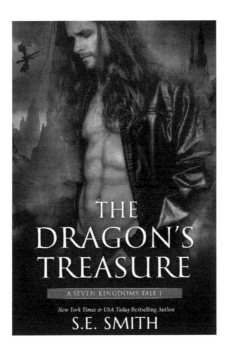

THE DRAGON'S TREASURE
*A Seven Kingdoms Tale*

Our story begins when the end is near, a portal is opened, and a curvy klutz stumbles on the last dragon left alive.

Once the King of the Isle of Dragons, Drago has now abandoned the emptiness of his realm and retreated, bitter and alone, to the caverns beneath the palace. In the form of his dragon, he remains hidden from the world, protecting the Dragon's Heart, the last legacy of his people —until he is disturbed by a most unlikely thief.

Carly Tate is determined to change something in her life. At first, the sudden storm during her trip to Yachats State Park seems like just another unlucky event drawn to her like a magnet—until, seeking shelter, she stumbles through a magical doorway! The cavern on the other side is filled with treasure, yet, as incredible as the piles of glittering gold and jewels are, her gaze is transfixed by the slumbering form of a magnificent dragon.

Eight books, Seven Kingdoms. A human woman will start a series of events that leads to an epic phenomenon! Can a centuries-old dragon protect his most valuable treasure, or will the evil that destroyed his race take Carly from him as well?

If you loved this story by me (Susan aka S.E. Smith) please leave a review! My websites are https://sesmithfl.com and https://sesmithya.com. Be sure to sign up for my newsletter to hear about new releases. Find your favorite way to keep in touch here: https://sesmithfl.com/contact-me/

RECOMMENDED READING ORDER LISTS:

https://sesmithfl.com/reading-list-by-events/

https://sesmithfl.com/reading-list-by-series/

MY GENRES:

## Contemporary / Romance

GIRLS FROM THE STREET

*She was born on the streets; he was born to rule.*

## Science Fiction / Romance

DRAGON LORDS OF VALDIER

*It all started with a king who crashed on Earth, desperately hurt. He inadvertently discovered a species that would save his own.*

CURIZAN WARRIOR

*The Curizans have a secret, kept even from their closest allies, but even they are not immune to the draw of a little known species from an isolated planet called Earth.*

MARASTIN DOW WARRIORS

*The Marastin Dow are reviled and feared for their ruthlessness, but not all want to live a life of murder. Some wait for just the right time to escape….*

SARAFIN WARRIORS

*A hilariously ridiculous human family who happen to be quite formidable… and a secret hidden on Earth. The origin of the Sarafin species is more than it seems. Those cat-shifting aliens won't know what hit them!*

DRAGONLINGS OF VALDIER NOVELLAS

*The Valdier, Sarafin, and Curizan Lords had children who just cannot stop getting into trouble! There is nothing as cute or funny as magical, shapeshifting kids, and nothing as heartwarming as family.*

## Cosmos' Gateway

*Cosmos created a portal between his lab and the warriors of Prime. Discover new worlds, new species, and outrageous adventures as secrets are unraveled and bridges are crossed.*

## The Alliance

*When Earth received its first visitors from space, the planet was thrown into a panicked chaos. The Trivators came to bring Earth into the Alliance of Star Systems, but now they must take control to prevent the humans from destroying themselves. No one was prepared for how the humans will affect the Trivators, though, starting with a family of three sisters....*

## Lords of Kassis

*It began with a random abduction and a stowaway, and yet, somehow, the Kassisans knew the humans were coming long before now. The fate of more than one world hangs in the balance, and time is not always linear....*

## Zion Warriors

*Time travel, epic heroics, and love beyond measure. Sci-fi adventures with heart and soul, laughter, and awe-inspiring discovery...*

## Rings of Power

*A powerful mage princess and her beloved stone dragon use her father's Rings of Power to explore new worlds—and find a safe haven when danger threatens their existence.*

**Paranormal / Fantasy / Romance**

## Magic, New Mexico

*Within New Mexico is a small town named Magic, an... <u>unusual</u> town, to say the least. With no beginning and no end, spanning genres, authors, and universes, hilarity and drama combine to keep you on the edge of your seat!*

## Spirit Pass

*There is a physical connection between two times. Follow the stories of those who travel back and forth. These westerns are as wild as they come!*

## SECOND CHANCE

*Stand-alone worlds featuring a woman who remembers her own death. Fiery and mysterious, these books will steal your heart.*

## MORE THAN HUMAN

*Long ago there was a war on Earth between shifters and humans. Humans lost, and today they know they will become extinct if something is not done….*

## THE FAIRY TALE SERIES

*A twist on your favorite fairy tales!*

## A SEVEN KINGDOMS TALE

*Long ago, a strange entity came to the Seven Kingdoms to conquer and feed on their life force. It found a host, and she battled it within her body for centuries while destruction and devastation surrounded her. Our story begins when the end is near, and a portal is opened….*

## Epic Science Fiction / Action Thrillers

### PROJECT GLIESE 581G

*An international team leave Earth to investigate a mysterious object in our solar system that was clearly made by someone, someone who isn't from Earth. Discover new worlds and conflicts in a sci-fi adventure sure to become your favorite!*

## New Adult / Young Adult

### BREAKING FREE

*A journey that will challenge everything she has ever believed about herself as danger reveals itself in sudden, heart-stopping moments.*

### THE DUST SERIES

*Fragments of a comet hit Earth, and Dust wakes to discover the world as he knew it is gone. It isn't the only thing that has changed, though, so has Dust…*

# About the Author

S.E. Smith is an *internationally acclaimed, New York Times* **and USA TODAY** *Bestselling* author of science fiction, romance, fantasy, paranormal, and contemporary works for adults, young adults, and children. She enjoys writing a wide variety of genres that pull her readers into worlds that take them away.

Printed in Great Britain
by Amazon

36458484R00077